IT CAME FROM THE WOODS

MATTHEW MERCER

For My Mother

"If we keep goofing off like this, we will never find Bigfoot."

Preface

I'll start this with a general content warning. My books may contain graphic descriptions of death, gore, nudity, sexual situations, and many other potentially offensive situations. To keep from spoiling the contents of *this* book, I won't guarantee that everything listed above will be inside, but it might. If any of this offends you, or if you are uncomfortable with your child reading a story containing these contents, this might not be the book for you or them. Otherwise, enjoy the story.

Acknowledgement

I would first like to thank anyone that has ever watched a horror movie with me. I wish I could name all of you, but I can't. Sorry.

I would like to thank anyone who purchased or read It Came From Above. Creating a story and sharing it with the world is a special feeling, and you guys make it possible for me.

For that same reason, I would like to thank you, whoever you are, for taking time out of your day to pick this book up(or opening it on a mobile device) and reading it.

I would like to thank my Father-In-Law, Raul, for the tremendous amount of support he gave me on that project. Without it, I don't know if I would be as confident with this next one.

I would like to thank my parents that support me in every way they can, including my mother Kimberly, who would be too frightened to read much further than her dedication page. If you've gotten this far I'm proud of you.

I'm gonna send some shout-outs to the guys that happened to be around me enough to be worth a mention. Jonathan, Kevin,

Jesse, Manny, Martin. Congratulations, your names made it into a book.

Lastly, shout-out to my wife, Natasha, who put up with my writing process while I should've been helping plan the wedding. You will forever be my biggest supporter. Thank you.

Contents

Chapter 1

Opening Interview

"Are you ready for this?" The interviewer asked behind the camera.

"As ready as I can be." Nancy sat upright in her favorite La-Z-Boy chair and pulled her water bottle to her lips. Her nerves were on edge. Her hand shook enough to miss her mouth with a few drops of water as she took a sip. The drops formed a small stream that traveled from her chin to her chest, disappearing beneath her shirt. "Is it recording already?" She looked past the camera to the interviewer that would question her for the duration of the documentary.

"Yes, it is." The man sounded young and confident.

She pulled her right leg over her left and clasped her fingers together, holding her right knee. She forced a smile. "Where do we start?"

"Why don't you introduce yourself?"

"Right." She pulled her bangs away from her forehead to behind her left ear. "Of course." She adjusted her top and swatted at the water on her chest. She looked directly into the camera. "Well, my name is Nancy Miller. Some of you might already know of me or have at least heard about what happened to me.

But for those of you who haven't," She shook her head, "you're in for a ride." She looked away from the camera, back toward the interviewer. "How was that?"

"That was perfect."

Nancy smiled and took another sip of water, this time much larger.

"Now, was there anything else you wanted to say before we rolled the footage?" He asked.

Nancy's eyes widened. With her mouth full of water, she put her bottle down and finished gulping. "Yeah, I guess so." She looked back at the camera. "The events you are about to witness are real. I know this footage has since leaked on the internet over the years, drawing all kinds of opinions about what may or may not have actually happened. Some call the footage edited, most call it fake, and a few of you might have believed it. But I'm here to tell you that this is real. This is my own collection of the tapes. No one has touched them until now. I haven't even watched them myself. On top of that, I have a complete say over what they do with the tapes here, so no, I will not let them edit them, even for the sake of the documentary. Everything you are about to see will be exactly as it happened. Even the parts that I'm not so proud to show."

"Is there any particular reason you are so adamant about getting the truth out there?"

She nodded her head, 'yes.' "I have spent my entire adult life defending myself over this situation. People have called me a liar and an attention whore. Hell, I've even been accused as the murderer of my friends! I've had to put up with this disrespect for too long now. This is the best way to give my side of the story. I know there will still be those who say it's fake, and that's fine. But this is my last option. I won't be able to stress about opinions anymore, knowing that I've done everything I can. And hopefully, once this is done, maybe I can finally get closure on this chapter in my life and move on to the next."

"Then let's get started."

Chapter 2

The Night Before

Camera 1

"Alright, how does this thing work?" A man said beneath muffled sounds that come with fondling a camera. The footage was all black until he yanked off the camera's lens cover, revealing a man sitting in the driver's seat of a truck. Various fishing rods, tents, and folding chairs occupying the truck bed were visible through the rear windshield.

Nancy: *Wow, look at him. He looks so pale.*

Interviewer: *Is that how you remember him?*

Nancy: *It must be the camera quality.*

"There we go. Is it rolling?" He fumbled with the camera until a look of confirmation lit up his face. "Sweet!" With the camera in hand, he reached over his steering wheel and placed it on the dash, adjusting it until it faced him. He turned his key in the ignition, put the van into gear, and began reversing his way out of his parking spot.

"Alright, so!" He clapped his hands on the steering wheel. "Our friend Winston has been working on this essay for a while now, but he has struggled with the material. I figured, why not go straight to the source and find the material ourselves? So, we sent out invites, planned a trip, and we are going on a full, week-long camping trip straight into the woods. What I didn't tell them was...." He took his right hand off the steering wheel and reached into his passenger seat, from which you could hear the sounds of a plastic bag ruffling from just outside the camera's view. He pulled into the camera's view a box containing another brand-new camera. "...we are going to be filming and documenting the entire thing."

Nancy: *Yeah. That was so unnecessary*

Interviewer: *What do you mean?*

Nancy: *He always had to go that extra mile. Honestly, I don't know if Winston was struggling with his essay. But Michael just **had** to make a camping trip out of it. And, of course, that wasn't enough either. I mean, a documentary? Really? None of us knew the first thing about making a documentary. It's all just so ridiculous, looking back on it now.*

Interviewer: *From that description, he sounds like he was at least a fun guy to be around. The type to never let you get bored, right?*

Nancy: *He was a dick. Sorry, can I say that?*

Interviewer: *The viewer will see many inappropriate things in the footage. Say what you like.*

Nancy: *Okay. He was a dick. He would make it seem like he did these things to help others, like Winston, but he only did it to stroke his ego. He just wanted to be the center of attention. He was a total dick.*

Interviewer: *So, would now be a proper time to share your relation to Michael with the audience?*

Nancy: *It's as good a time as any. He was my boyfriend.*

Michael put the unopened camera back in his passenger seat. "I got four cameras. Assuming we all take turns, it should be enough for everyone." He leaned in and narrowed his eyes as he focused on the road briefly. He turned the wheel and made a left turn, never making any attempt to turn on his signal. Once he seemed to be on a straightaway, he continued. "Now, I'm sure those watching this footage in the future are probably asking yourself, what is this all about? What is Winston's topic? Why would it ever be so important that it would warrant a documentary? Why am I even watching this?" He took his eyes off the road to look straight into the camera. "Well, let me tell you. We are going on the hunt for the one and only Bigfoot." He looked back toward the road. "Or Sasquatch, whichever you prefer. We are heading as deep into the woods as our young bodies will allow us. Straight into dangerous lands, far from any human reach, looking for the first ever indisputable proof that this legendary creature exists."

Interviewer: *So, do you think you did?*

Nancy: *Did what?*

Interviewer: *Do you think you found indisputable proof that Bigfoot exists?*

Nancy: *Indisputable? No. Forty years later, people still deny it. But I'll let the footage speak for itself.*

"So, tonight, the whole crew is coming to our apartment. We are gonna get drunk, you know, party a little bit," he held two fingers to his lips, pretending to smoke a joint "have ourselves a good time and get ready for our little road trip tomorrow." As he finished talking, he shifted his car into park and unbuckled his seat belt.

He grabbed the camera off the dashboard and pointed it toward the passenger seat, where the camera he showed off earlier sat next to an opened, empty camera box and a plastic bag from RadioShack containing two additional unopened cameras. "I got all the cameras here." The footage shook as he put the other camera back in the bag, grabbed the bag from the seat , and got out of the car. He brought the camera around to the back of the truck to show off the fishing rods, tents, and other camping gear. "We've got most of our stuff for the trip already packed back here. All that's left is getting the crew together with our personal belongings." He pointed the camera at the large apartment building. It was freshly painted a clean beige color accented with a dark brown roof. A large tree sat right outside in the grass, to the left of the stairs that Michael would soon climb. "It's not much, but it's home."

Nancy: *God, this brings back memories.*

Interviewer: *Good memories?*

Nancy: *Some good, some not so good.*

Interviewer: *Care to enlighten us?*

Nancy: *Well, this was our apartment. And as I'm sure you know, relationships have their ups and downs. But this was the first place I lived outside of my parents' house, and it was my first time being in a serious relationship like this. So, naturally, there were some great memories.*

Interviewer: *Like this next scene?*

Nancy: *It would've been a better memory if it wasn't leaked on the internet.*

"Nancy!" Michael yelled upon entering the apartment. He walked through the kitchen to drop the bag of cameras on the small dining table, then made his way through the apartment, stopping just outside a bedroom door as the camera picked up the sound of rushing shower water. Michael looked into the camera with a mischievous smile. As he entered the bedroom, he aimed the camera at a trail of clothes on the floor that led to the bathroom. The trail started with a dark t-shirt, then a pair of blue jeans with one inside-out leg, then a mismatched set of women's underwear and bra, and lastly, a pair of socks.

He entered the bathroom, that the scalding shower water filled with steam. He pointed the camera at the fogged-up glass shower door, through which you could see a vague silhouette of a naked, auburn-haired girl lathering up one leg that she placed on the outside of the tub. Michael pointed the camera toward himself and held up one finger to his mouth as if telling the viewers to 'shush' while the girl in the shower was humming a song.

Interviewer: *Do you remember what song you were humming?*

Nancy: *"Don't You Want Me" by The Human League*

Interviewer: *A personal favorite of yours?*

Nancy: *At the time.*

Interviewer: *Do you always sing in the shower?*

Nancy: *I used to. Now, only when I'm having a good week, and that's rare.*

Michael positioned the camera on a counter and aimed it toward the shower, where he briefly waited with his hand on the door. When Nancy put her leg back down to rinse it off, he slid the door wide open and yelled, "Boo!"

Nancy shrieked and fell to the floor. She stopped screaming once she recognized that it was Michael, but the fear hadn't left her eyes. "You're such an asshole!" She yelled, smacking his hand that he offered to help pull her up. She stood up of her own volition. "You scared the hell out of me!" She hit him in the chest, but Michael was unfazed.

Nancy: *Remember when I said he's a dick?*

Interviewer: *I remember.*

Nancy: *Total dick.*

Interviewer: *I- I can't argue with that.*

"Come on, let me make it up to you." Michael pushed the shower head away from Nancy, who looked too stunned to move. He grabbed a towel and wrapped her in it, though her hair was still completely covered in either shampoo or conditioner, if not both. He then grabbed both ends of the towel, unraveled the front, and used it to pull her body to his and kiss her. She no longer seemed mad at him as she wore a huge smile while she kissed him back. He grabbed her face with his left hand and used his right to remove the towel and throw it to the floor beneath him.

Interviewer: *I'm assuming it's footage like this that you mentioned you weren't too proud to show off.*

Nancy: *This isn't even the worst of it.*

Interviewer: *Be that as it may, we can still at least censor the footage. Nobody would fault you for that.*

Nancy: *No. As I mentioned, this footage needs to remain* **completely** *unedited. Besides, most of this stuff has already leaked on the internet. If I try to hide it here, it's only gonna drive those weird perverts to seek the footage elsewhere.*

As Michael ran his hands up and down her body, things got more physical as she seemingly attacked his face with her own. However, it only took her opening a single eye for just a second to ruin the moment.

"Uh, what is that?" She asked.

"You can feel it already?" He asked while he unzipped his pants.

"No," she pushed him off her and pointed at the camera with one hand while she covered up as much of herself as possible with the other, "that!"

"Oh, that? Do you like it? We could make a movie." He leaned back in for another kiss, but she put her hand in front of his face to stop him.

"Well, you thought wrong." She closed the shower door and readjusted the shower head to point it back to herself. "Now get out of here. You lost your chance."

"You're no fun." He walked to the camera, picked it up, and looked straight into the lens. "By the end of the week, I promise we'll get some quality footage." He winked before turning the camera off.

Interviewer: *I know you've said he's a dick, but I couldn't help but notice the smile you had watching that scene.*

Nancy: *He had his moments. I was young. He was attractive. It wasn't always bad.*

***

Camera 1

When the camera is turned back on, Nancy is seen looking into the camera with Michael behind her shoulder.

"There you go." He said.

"It's recording?" Nancy asked.

"Yep. Easy, right?"

"Yeah, I guess so." Nancy waved the camera around the room. It was the same bedroom that Michael had entered earlier. The two of them were seated on a large, at least queen-sized bed. Nancy was fully clothed, and her mess of clothes on the floor had since been replaced by a wet towel. The footage was directed toward the door as a doorbell drew Nancy's attention to the front of the house.

"People are here already?" Michael asked. "What time is it?"

"I think it's just after four." Nancy brought the camera with her as she hopped off of the bed.

"Seriously? Where did the time go?"

"RadioShack." Nancy followed Michael to the front door.

He opened it, and they greeted a tall Hispanic man who looked the same age as them. Michael was rather tall himself, but this man was even taller. However, Michael had more clear muscular bulk.

Nancy: *Daniel Hernandez. Always the first to arrive.*

Interviewer: *I see you rolling your eyes. Do you consider that to be a bad trait?*

Nancy: *Not **that**, exactly. But his overall personality could sometimes be annoying.*

Interviewer: *Can you elaborate?*

Nancy: *Well, his dad was a cop, and he would act like he was, too.*

Interviewer: *And he wasn't?*

Nancy: *No. He was either in training or going to school for it. I don't remember. But, he just carried himself around like he was better than you for it—a real stickler for the rules type of guy.*

"Daniel! It's good to see you." Michael said.

"It's good to see you guys, too! What's up, Nancy?" Daniel noticed the camera while he gave Michael a half-high-five-half-hug, standing outside the front door. "What's this? Are you guys filming?

"It's a long story," Nancy said from behind the camera.

"Not just us. Everyone is." Michael said, drawing an eyebrow raise from Daniel.

"Who is everyone?"

"You, me, her," Michael pointed past the camera to Nancy, "everyone else that shows up. We are making a documentary!"

"What about Bigfoot?" Daniel looked significantly less excited about it than Michael was. "You guys don't think we're actually going to find something, do you?"

"Of course, we will." Michael said, looking into the camera with a face that screamed, 'is this guy serious?'

"At the very least, it will be fun. Recording the whole thing." Nancy said.

"If you say so." Daniel's face lit up as he looked down the stairs toward the sound of another person walking up the stairs. "Who do we have here?" He stepped out of the way, allowing a girl to enter the doorway.

"Hi." She said to Daniel with a smile. She was much shorter than him, about five-foot-four, and had pitch-black hair. She wore black latex pants and a rocker-style fur jacket.

"Bianca!" Nancy squealed and ran to her. The footage was shaky and unclear while they hugged, which was only discernible once they pulled away from each other. "I'm so glad you could make it."

"Me, too!" Bianca said.

Interviewer: *Alright, why don't you tell us about Bianca?*

Nancy: *She's the best. We go way, way back.*

Interviewer: *How did you guys meet?*

Nancy: *Her parents were friends with mine growing up. If I'm being honest with you, she's probably my oldest friend. We used to do everything together, spending all of our time at each other's houses and going on camping trips with each other* **constantly**. *That is until she moved to New Jersey before high school.*

Interviewer: *She doesn't look like the camping type.*

Nancy: *She used to be. I hadn't seen her for so long, and I thought this would be the perfect opportunity to reconnect! But, yeah, I admit, when she first walked to my door, I thought the same thing. She was just so pretty. I wasn't used to seeing her like that.*

Interviewer: *She wasn't always that pretty?*

Nancy: *Goodness, no. Not when we were kids, at least. She was more of the tomboyish type. But that girl on the camera? I would've*

*bet every dollar I had that she would get in a car and drive away
the second she got some dirt on her nails.*

Interviewer: *Did you keep in touch when she moved? Letters,
phone calls, anything?*

Nancy: *We would call each other for a while during freshman
year, but it stopped after a while. We must've grown apart. I was
so happy to hear her when she called and said she was moving back
home!*

"My name's Daniel. Daniel Hernandez." Daniel extended his
hand to Bianca.

"Is this your boyfriend, Nancy? He's cute." Her eyes opened
wide as she looked toward Nancy and shook Daniel's hand.

"No, this is my boyfriend, Michael." The camera showed
Nancy's hand reaching out and grabbing Michael's shoulder.

Michael offered his hand to her. "Nice to meet you."

"Well, there are cute guys all over this place, aren't there?"
Bianca said, taking her time to take her eyes off Daniel to shake
Michael's hand. "And look at you, girl!" Bianca waved her hands
in the outline of an hourglass toward Nancy.

"No, look at you! I can hardly even recognize you anymore."
Nancy said.

Nancy: *I admit, I thought it would be much easier to rekindle
that friendship we used to have. I thought things would've just
clicked together, but she seemed like a different person. It was like
I was meeting her all over again. I remember staying up late*

at night, the same blanket wrapped around our shoulders as we roasted marshmallows over a campfire. We would have all kinds of mud stains on our pants and smell like fish from our mornings spent catching them with our parents. But something about her just felt different.

Interviewer: *So you'd say there was some sort of disconnect there?*

Nancy: *Exactly! This girl looks like she had never even eaten a marshmallow in her life! She looked like one of those fashion models you'd see on a magazine cover. I couldn't imagine her letting a single speck of dirt touch her shoes, let alone her clothing. And talking about boys being cute? The way she was checking out Daniel? That is **not** the girl I remembered. But I'd like to think that throughout the trip, the rekindling happened. Just not as immediately as I had assumed it would.*

"So, are you gonna let us in or not?" Daniel asked, drawing a laugh from Bianca.

"Oh, yes, of course!" Michael stepped out of the way so they could enter the apartment, and Nancy led them to the living room.

"This is where you guys will be sleeping. We only have these two couches, so I'll let you guys fight over them. We have a lot of blankets that we were going to pull out, so one of you could make a bed on the floor as well." Nancy said.

There was another knock on the door.

As Nancy walked to the front, the camera caught Bianca whispering something into Daniel's ear that made him smile, but the camera couldn't pick up what she had said.

Nancy opened the door to a man that wasn't quite as tall as Michael but wasn't short by any means. His hair was messy, and his glasses crooked on his face. He wore dirty boots, pants that were too big for him, and a graphic t-shirt that was too tight on him, along with a backpack overflowing with obviously heavy textbooks.

"What's with the camera?" He said, without any other greeting.

"Oh, you're gonna love this!" Michael appeared in the frame from behind the camera. "I thought, for your Bigfoot project, why don't we turn it into a documentary?"

"That's stupid. It has to be an essay. It's for English class." The man invited himself inside the apartment, stepping between Michael and the camera.

Nancy: *That's Winston. Winston Pence. The man of the hour. Don't mind him. He kind of lacks basic social skills.*

Interviewer: *I wasn't going to say anything.*

Nancy: *He's missing quite a few screws in his head, but he means well.*

The camera followed Winston to the dining room table, where he dropped off his backpack and spotted the other camera's that Michael had bought. "Oh, you bought more cameras?"

"Yeah, what's the deal with those, anyways?" Bianca asked from the living room, where she was now sitting next to Daniel.

"Winston here is writing an essay on Bigfoot for class. I'm sure Nancy must've mentioned that when she invited you." Michael said.

"She mentioned something like that, I think. So why the cameras?" Bianca said.

"I don't get it, either," Winston said, shaking his head.

"Well, we are going to document our entire trip. I hope we will catch some nice footage Winston could use to reference in his essay." Michael said.

"So, you expect us just to film everything while we're out there?" Bianca said.

"Exactly." Michael reached into the RadioShack bag, pulled out all the unopened cameras, and brought them into the living room. He sat on the couch opposite Daniel and Bianca.

Nancy followed, only to sit on the floor with the camera in her lap.

"I'll show you how to use them once everyone gets here. I just don't want to go over it more than once. I want everyone to take turns using them, never turning them off unless you are going to sleep. Record the whole trip, and maybe one of us will get Bigfoot on film." Michael said.

"Sounds like fun," Bianca said.

"Thank you! And these are nice cameras, too. They've got that new night-vision feature, so we can even record at night time." Michael said.

"Okay, *that's* cool," Winston spoke loudly from the dining room.

"Right? I thought so." Michael stood up. "Can I get you guys anything? Beer? Soda?"

"I'll take a beer-"

"Soda for me, thanks," Winston said, interrupting Bianca, who had annoyance written all over her face.

"Beer. Thank you." Bianca finished her sentence.

"Got it. Daniel, what about you-" Michael stopped short as he looked out of the glass sliding door to the porch. "Is there a fire outside?"

Nancy picked up the camera and brought it outside, right behind Michael. There was an extensive smoke trail coming from behind the balcony.

"Oh, these guys." Michael laughed. "No big deal, everybody." Michael waved to everyone that followed him to go back inside.

The smoke trail was coming from an all-white van parked outside. It was the kind of van that didn't have any back windows. The exact type that parents would teach young children to avoid. The only windows on the van were from the front two seats, cracked just enough to allow the smoke from inside to pour out.

Nancy: *We used to call that style a "rape van."*

Interviewer: *I'm pretty sure people still call them that.*

"You know them?" Bianca asked.

"Know them? They're coming on the trip with us." Michael said, walking to the front door.

Nancy followed Michael down the stairs and to the back of the van.

"Police, you're under arrest!" Michael yelled, swinging the back doors wide open.

Inside was a single couple: a guy and a girl. The girl screamed while the guy tried to throw his joint out of a nonexistent window, leaving burns on the shag carpet interior of his fan.

The girl wore a floral headband over her long, straight hair that flowed down her back to her butt. Her looks highlighted native roots, thanks to her darker-than-tan skin tone.

The guy looked to be rather dirty. He had oily skin, greasy hair, and dirt under his nails. He wore a leather vest without a shirt beneath it, along with faded blue jeans.

Interviewer: *So, tell me about them.*

Nancy: *Mitch and Alyssa. The obligatory stoners of our group. They were that couple where everyone adored the girl and thought that the boy didn't deserve her. I mean, she was beautiful. Stunning, even. But she wasted all of that once she got with Mitch. She would've been the prettiest of all of us if she had put in the effort, but she stopped believing in makeup because of "animal testing" or something to that effect. Lucky for her, she didn't need it. She just had that natural beauty going on.*

Interviewer: *You don't sound like a fan of Mitch.*

Nancy: *Don't get me wrong, I love him. But Alyssa was my friend first, and I can't help but think about how much better of a life she could've had if she had never met him and stayed on her own trajectory. And Mitch was never really sober enough for me to get a good read on him. He was always super fun, and made it hard to be mad at him, but he was just **so** dumb.*

"I think we've got all the video evidence we need," Nancy said.

"Fuck, you guys!" Alyssa grabbed the fuzzy pillow she had been leaning on and threw it at Michael.

Mitch appeared so far gone that he wasn't even sure where he was anymore. He just stared blankly at the camera while his mouth slowly grew more and more agape.

"Come on. We're just messing with you. Let's go inside, and I'll order a pizza." Michael said.

"Yeah, I'm sure they're hungry," Nancy said.

"And you might as well shut the camera off for now. We don't want to waste batteries before the trip starts."

After a bit of fumbling, the footage ended.

***

Camera 1

When Nancy turned on the camera again, she was seated on the couch next to Michael, Daniel, and Bianca. Winston was on the other couch alone while Alyssa and Mitch were sitting crisscrossed on the floor. There was an almost empty pizza box on the floor between them, and everybody seemed to be done with eating except for Winston, who had three slices of pizza stacked on top of each other on the couch without a plate.

"Alright, well, I'm glad everyone made it-" Michael started.

"Wait, this is all of us?" Winston interrupted.

"Yeah?" Nancy asked from behind the camera.

"What about Lauren? You guys told me she would be coming."

"She couldn't make it. Something about being sick, I don't know. You know how she is." Nancy said.

Nancy: *Lauren Richardson. She called me that day, coming up with a bunch of excuses to get out of the trip, which wasn't unusual for her.*

Interviewer: *She backed out of stuff a lot?*

Nancy: *Almost always. It was really hard to get her to do **anything**.*

"Anyways," Michael continued, "I just wanted to go over the plan for tomorrow. Once again, Winston here is writing his essay on Bigfoot. While studying, he came across some film that supposedly took place in this forest up North. That is where we will be heading. The footage they recorded was thirty seconds long and super blurry. I figured, let's document our little camping trip and come up with something better. Some real, hard, concrete evidence that Bigfoot is real. Whether we see one or not, this trip will be a lot of fun, and Winston can't write a bad paper on the topic after diving head-first into the creature's territory. I'm sure you've noticed the camera we've been carrying around." Michael pointed to the camera. "I bought a total of four of them. The plan is for each of us to document every single thing that occurs during this trip."

"Who knows? Maybe we will actually find something and get rich off of it." Daniel suggested.

Michael took the unopened cameras and handed one to Winston, Bianca, and Alyssa.

"What's that?" Mitch, who clearly wasn't sober enough to pay attention, asked.

"What, don't I get one?" Daniel asked.

"You and Bianca seem to be getting along nicely. Share." Michael said. "Now, are there any other questions?"

"Yeah, how do they work?" Winston asked, ripping his box open.

"Let me show you." Michael walked over to the camera that Nancy was holding and turned it off.

Nancy: *Not much else happened that night. Michael ensured everyone knew how to turn the cameras on and off and got to bed soon after.*

Chapter 3

Getting Ready

Camera 2

The earliest footage from that morning began with Bianca yawning, with which her throat emitted some quiet, high-pitched moans.

Nancy: *How was even her yawn adorable?*

Bianca slept in only what appeared to be some underwear bottoms that were unflattering, considering the kind that was common practice in the 80s, and a white tank top that wasn't see-through but was thin enough to show viewers that it had been a cold morning.

She pointed the camera at a sleeping Daniel sharing the couch with her. She stood up and aimed the camera at Mitch and Alyssa, who were sleeping on the floor. She stepped over them and stepped out onto the back porch. She propped the camera up on the table outside and pointed it at the chair she proceeded to sit on.

"Daniel snuck onto the couch with me in the middle of the night." She lit a cigarette and took a puff. "I thought it was cute until he started to snore—a real mood-killer, that one. Nothing happened, though. I promise, Nancy, your couch is clean."

Nancy: *That's good to know, I guess. I wonder where that couch even is today.*

"And what's up with that Winston guy? I mean, where'd you even find him? I kept catching him staring at me throughout the night. Mitch and Alyssa, though." She looked into the camera. "I *love* them. Mitch is so fun, even when he doesn't mean to be. And Alyssa is just the nicest person ever."

She ashed her cigarette and picked up the camera. "Alright, sorry for this." She brought the camera through the house and into Nancy's room without bothering to knock.

"Time to wake up!" She yelled, yanking the comforter off of Michael and Nancy.

Nancy immediately jumped out of bed, but Michael didn't seem to notice.

Nancy: *I still remember the rush of cold air attacking my thighs when she did that. I don't think I've slept a single day without locking my bedroom door since then.*

"Bianca? What the fuck? What time is it?" Nancy asked, clearly annoyed. A bedside alarm began to ring right behind where Nancy was now standing. She reached over and shut it off.

Michael rolled over. "How are you both up this early?" He asked, his eyes still closed.

"Couldn't sleep. Can I use your bathroom? Your other one is gross, and I don't wanna be in there for the full length of a shower." Bianca said. "Plus, I'm worried Winston would find a way to barge in on me."

"That's a logical fear." Michael sat up straight. "Just wait until you're camping with him for the next week."

"Yeah, you can use it. But don't take too long. We still need to get ready, and we've gotta hit the road soon." Nancy said.

"Thanks!" Bianca brought the camera back toward the living room, where she grabbed her maroon duffel bag from the corner behind the couch that Daniel was still sleeping on. She started heading back to Nancy's room. Once she passed the front door, the camera shook, and she gasped at the sound of someone knocking. She continued into Nancy's room.

"Somebody's knocking on the door." She said, walking right past Nancy on the bed and into the bathroom. She closed the door as she entered and dropped her bag on the toilet lid. She left the camera on the counter while she dug through her bag. She searched through a plethora of unconventional clothing for a camping trip before settling on a black and red floral sundress.

Interviewer: *Did I see a pink leotard in there?*

Nancy: *Hey, it was the 80s.*

Interviewer: *What, was she going to do aerobics in the woods?*

Nancy: *I wouldn't have put it past her.*

She hung the dress over the towel rack on the wall. While lifting the bottom of her tank top, she realized that the camera was still recording. "Nice try." She giggled and reached over to turn it off.

***

Camera 1

Nancy turned her camera on to record herself scrolling through her closet and picking out a red, satin robe. She threw it on and brought the camera to the front door, where that person was *still* knocking.

She swung the door open, revealing a Caucasian girl dressed in a preppy, white, collared blouse paired with a black skirt. An oversized suitcase was lying on its back next to her feet.

"Surprise!" She yelled, throwing her hands up and spilling coffee from her cup onto her suitcase but pretending not to notice.

Nancy: *And a surprise it was. That's Lauren. She was the last person I thought was at my door.*

"Changed your mind, huh?" Nancy said.

"Yeah, it's not too late, is it?" Lauren gave a teeth-showing smile.

"Definitely not. You're probably the only person that is ready to go right now. I think most of them are still sleeping, but come inside."

Lauren entered the apartment, and Nancy closed the door behind her.

Nancy led her through the kitchen to the dining room table, where Lauren jumped as she turned the corner.

"Jesus!" She yelled.

Alyssa and Mitch stood upright in the center of the living room, seemingly dressed and ready to go. Their sleeping bags were already rolled up and leaning against the wall.

Nancy: *I didn't think much of it then, but I don't recall hearing the guest shower before that moment.*

Daniel was stretching his arms out as if he was just waking up. He looked around the couch as if he were either looking for Bianca or unsure how he got there.

"Oh, good, you're all awake!" Nancy said. "Look who decided to tag along." The camera motioned over to Lauren.

She put her suitcase next to the table and sat down, laying her face between her arms.

Nancy brought the camera back into her bedroom. "You getting ready, babe?" She asked Michael, who was digging through their dresser.

"I will be as soon as that friend of yours gets out of our bathroom. Is anyone else ready?" He asked.

"Lauren is, apparently."

"Lauren?"

"Yeah, she just got here, dressed and ready to go. Mitch and Alyssa are both ready. Daniel just woke up. I haven't seen Winston."

"Geez. It's way too early even to function right now." Michael said.

Nancy knocked on the bathroom door. "Bianca? You almost done?" The camera wasn't picking up the sound of any shower water.

"Yeah, almost! You guys can come in and shower if you're ready!" Bianca yelled through the door.

"I think we'll just wait," Nancy said.

***

Camera 3

The camera turns on and features Alyssa sparking up a joint in the same seat on the back porch that Bianca smoked in earlier. She wore cutoff denim shorts and an oversized gray pullover hoodie with sleeves that hung down to her fingertips.

"This won't get me in trouble, will it?" Alyssa asked, trying to hide the joint from the camera while she took a hit.

"Only if the cops get the footage. Should I send it to them?" Mitch asked from behind the camera.

He was joking, but Alyssa looked paranoid at the thought. Either way, it didn't hold her back from hitting it again.

"I'll make extra sure to send it to them if you don't pass that over here!" He laughed hysterically as his hand entered the frame.

She flipped him off and took a long, two-second puff before slamming it into his open palm and storming back inside the apartment.

Mitch turned the camera around to face himself. "I think I scared her." He said and took a hit from the joint. He had a straight, serious look on his face for a brief moment before he cracked and broke into an outrageous roar of laughter.

Nancy: *I knew they did it in their car, and it shouldn't surprise me, but they could've gotten me evicted if they got caught doing that on my porch.*

The rest of the footage featured Mitch smoking and blowing ring-shaped smoke clouds between alternating coughing and laughing fits.

***

Camera 4

The camera turned on to a very unkempt Winston, sitting on the couch looking straight into the lens while Lauren took a nap on the couch next to him. "Alright, it is officially..." he scanned the room until he settled on the wall clock directly behind him, "...eight o'clock in the morning. I think the majority of us are almost ready to leave and get this trip started. Michael apparently thought it was a good idea to turn this trip into a documentary, and I have to admit, I could use a record of source material for this essay, so why the hell not? And what is a documentary without personal interviews? I figure I'll start."

Lauren let out one loud snore that caused Winston to stare at her for about five seconds in silence.

He picked up the camera and took it into the kitchen with him, where Alyssa already was.

"What's going on?" Alyssa asked while she stuffed her face with a poppy-seed muffin.

"It's an interview," Winston said.

"Okay." Alyssa waited a few seconds. "So ... aren't you gonna ask me a question?"

"Right. Are you excited about the trip?" Winston asked her.

"More or less."

"Come on. You've gotta give me more than that."

She placed her muffin on the counter with a certain passive aggressiveness. "I'm not a big fan of road trips, but I am a fan of the wilderness. I'm excited to be away from the grips of society for a week. I like the thought of telling stories by the fire, getting my feet dirty, and bathing in an open lake. I'm not excited about the back pain from poor sleeping posture or having to squat in a bush to take a piss." She crossed her arms. "How was that?"

"Perfect." Winston put a thumbs-up in front of the camera lens. "So what do you think? Is Bigfoot real?"

Alyssa choked on the coffee that she was sipping. She leaned over the counter and used her left hand to wipe away any spilled onto her face.

"Damn, are you okay?" Winston asked.

"I'll be fine." She waved him off with her other hand to signal that she was okay.

"Maybe take smaller gulps next time."

Alyssa gave the camera an annoyed look. "Sorry, what was your question?"

"Bigfoot! What do you think? Is he real? Will we see one?"

"Oh, right. Well, I don't know. I don't see why he can't be real, but I could also see people making up something stupid like that. Either way, I hope we will see *some* cool wildlife on our trip.

"Alright, thanks, Alyssa!"

She smiled at him.

"I'll have plenty of questions for you throughout the trip, but this was a great start," Winston said.

Her smile faded, and her eyes rolled just as she went out of frame.

"Let's see, who's next?" He whispered into the camera.

Bianca walked past him with her sundress on, but her hair was still a mess, and her makeup hadn't been started yet.

"Bianca! How about an interview?" Winston shoved the camera entirely too close to her face.

She was caught off guard but managed to cover her face as soon as she spotted the camera. "Ew, no!" She pushed the camera away.

Winston managed to take the hint and point it at himself instead. He wore a confused expression on his face. He pointed the camera at the bedroom door as he approached it and knocked.

Michael opened it as he was putting on an all-white t-shirt. "What's up?" he asked.

"I'm interviewing everyone for the documentary. You're up next." Winston said.

"Oh?" Michael seemed excited that somebody was finally taking his documentary idea seriously. He opened the door wider and invited him in. Michael ran to the bathroom door, where the shower water could be heard running, and shut the door.

"Alright, so let's get started." Winston took a seat on the floor while Michael continued to walk about the room to finish packing. "So, are you excited about the trip?"

"Uhmm," Michael thought about the question while loosely throwing unfolded clothes into his stuffed duffel bag, "I'm not excited about driving for five hours."

"I see a pattern here so far. Nobody is excited about the road trip."

"If we all fit into one car, it would probably be more fun. Maybe if we had an RV, but that wasn't going to happen."

"Fair point," Winston said. You could hear that the shower water had stopped running. "So, what about Bigfoot? Is he real?"

"Come on, really? If a species as big as this one is described was out in the wilderness, we would've discovered it by now."

"But you went through the whole process of documenting this trip?"

"Yeah, because if he *is* real, we will make a shit ton of money. And if he *isn't* real, I still have these cool-ass cameras." Michael pointed toward the camera

Nancy: *I think throughout this entire trip, that was the only time where Michael admits that it was a money thing.*

Interviewer: *He never said anything to you?*

Nancy: *Nope.*

The bathroom door opened, and Michael leaned back to look inside. "Okay, the interview is over. She's gotta get dressed."

Winston got off the floor and brought the camera out of the room. The bedroom door could be heard closing behind him.

Winston brought the camera back into the living room, where Daniel was chatting up Bianca.

Daniel must have just gotten out of the shower as he only wore a towel around his waist.

Bianca seemed to pay him no mind as she put on her makeup with a palm-sized mirror in her hand.

"Daniel, you're up!" Winston said.

Daniel turned around, annoyed. "What?"

"I'm interviewing everyone before we leave. You're next."

Daniel took a seat next to Bianca on the couch.

"Oh, I thought you would get dressed first," Winston said.

"I'm still drying off. Come on, let's make this quick."

"Uhm, okay." Winston cleared his throat. "Do you think we're gonna find Bigfoot?"

"I hope so." He pats Bianca on the back, almost causing her to ruin her makeup. "What do you think?"

"I hope we don't! I mean, what do we do if we see one? Kill it?" Bianca said.

"We get rich! We will sell this documentary for millions of dollars, and we'd never have to work a day again. Fuck the police academy." Daniel uncrossed his legs, coming within inches of exposing himself beneath the towel to the camera.

"Alright, well, that's all for now!" Winston got up with a hustle and headed to the back porch.

Nancy: *There's no way that Winston didn't see his whole dick just then.*

Interviewer: *It sure would seem that way.*

Winston adjusted the camera on the table so he could look into it as he continued filming. "These interviews were pretty unimpressive, but I'm hopeful we will get better ones throughout the week.

"What?" An unidentified voice called out from behind the camera, causing Winston to jump out of his seat.

"Fuck, dude!" Winston yelled. "I didn't even see you there. Winston turned the camera around to find Mitch still seated in his chair from earlier, his camera in his lap. "Do you mind if I interview you quickly?" Winston asked.

After a few seconds passed, Mitch broke the silence. "What?"

"Yeah, that's enough for the interviews right now." Winston turned the camera back to himself. Disappointment stretched across his face as he shut the camera off.

***

Camera 2

The camera now featured Bianca on the couch, still doing her makeup.

Daniel got up from the couch and grabbed the camera from where she had positioned it. "Come on. The viewers want to see a Sasquatch, not your makeup routine!"

She shot him an evil look.

Nancy: *If looks could kill, Jesus.*

Daniel held the camera with one hand while he grabbed his suitcase for the trip with his other and proceeded out of the apartment. "We're losing daylight, people!" He yelled back into the door that he had left open.

Nancy: *He was essentially the last person to wake up, but the second he finishes getting ready, he starts rushing everybody else.*

He positioned the camera on the bed of Michael's truck in time to catch everyone else following shortly behind him while he placed his suitcase in the bed.

Nobody looked particularly happy about this part of the trip, most notably Lauren, who looked like a zombie.

Nancy: *Mornings were never her thing. Poor girl.*

"So I take it you're riding with us, then?" Michael said to Daniel as he put his own bags in the truck.

"You're damn right. I don't trust them-" Daniel pointed to Mitch and Alyssa, who were putting their bags in the back of their van just across the parking lot behind them, "-enough to drive. I want to live through this trip, personally."

"I'm with you, too." Bianca appeared in the frame, seemingly out of nowhere, with a giant suitcase she tossed over Michael's head into the truck.

It scared Michael, his face looked quite disturbed, but he kept it to himself.

"I didn't come on this trip to ride with strangers." Bianca finished.

"Fair enough," Michael said.

Daniel picked up the camera and focused it on Winston, who was peeking into the truck's bed, which now lacked space for another bag.

"Put your stuff in the van. We can't fit any more people in my truck, so you've gotta ride with Mitch." Michael said.

Winston leaned his head back and looked at the clouds in frustration. "Seriously?"

"Yeah, dude. Sorry. And you can tell Lauren over there the same thing. At least she can keep you company."

Winston pulled his bag off the ground in a passive-aggressive fashion, muttering under his breath while walking toward Lauren.

"I guess he didn't like that, did he?" Daniel said.

"He'll get over it. Look at him." Michael pointed just out of frame.

Daniel followed with the camera, pointing it toward Winston, who was already smiling from ear to ear while he talked to an unenthused Lauren.

"See, now he gets to spend an extended period of time with a woman," Michael said.

"You did the right thing," Daniel said.

"Poor girl," Bianca said from out of frame.

Daniel brought the camera to her.

"Not only is she stuck with him, but those idiots too." Bianca directed the camera toward the van where Mitch and Alyssa were giggling hysterically.

"Oh, here she comes!" Michael yelled.

Daniel pointed the camera at Nancy as she locked the apartment with her bags in hand and descended the stairs.

"Finally! What took you so long?" Daniel yelled.

Nancy only responded with a middle finger from her hand that was holding the keys.

Nancy: *It was still way too early for me to deal with their shit*

"Is everyone ready? Do you guys have everything? Clothing? Toiletries? Cameras?" Michael scanned the group, now gathered in a large circle in the center of the parking lot.

Nobody objected.

"Then let's get going. Roll those cameras during the road trip. We've got extra batteries that I snuck into Winston's bag last night, so don't worry about that. I gave Alyssa the directions, but Mitch, just follow closely behind me. If I notice you are no longer behind me, I will pull over at the next gas station and wait for you." Michael said.

A brief silence followed.

"What?" Mitch finally said, warranting groans from the group and a look of lost hope from Winston.

"Don't worry. I'm driving." Alyssa held up the keys to the van.

Lauren and Winston exhaled, visibly loosening up as their shoulders fell.

Mitch just giggled.

Nancy: *Alyssa wasn't necessarily sober, but at least she was on the same planet as the rest of us.*

Chapter 4

Road Trip

Camera 2

The first few hours of footage from the road trip were slow. Nancy would spend most of the time sleeping in the passenger seat, and Daniel passed out as soon as the car left the apartment complex, leaving Bianca in charge of the camera. She insisted on shutting it off multiple times, but Michael insisted on leaving it on "in case something happens."

"But the camera keeps shaking." She would say.

Nancy: *You could feel every single bump in the road with Michael's truck. It made everything super uncomfortable. I wish I could say I got a good rest during this road trip, but I'm only half asleep there.*

"It will be fine." He would insist.

She tried her best to record through the windows and capture the open road, but none of the footage was great due to the shaking.

Bianca and Michael shared subtle small talk here and there, but Bianca was mainly pestering him about his relationship with Nancy.

"Where'd you guys meet?"

"Where was the first date?"

"How long did it take you guys to move in together?"

"What was the first thing you noticed about her?

His replies were simple and could have been more interesting.

"In High School."

"The movies."

"As soon as we graduated."

"Her ass."

Nancy rolled in her seat following that last response, causing Michael to rethink his answer.

"Or, maybe it was her red hair."

All the while these conversations were happening, Michael's *journey* tape was repeatedly playing through the speakers. He would repeat "Don't Stop Believin'" twice on each listen before allowing the next song to play.

Bianca would groan from behind the camera each time. When the song came around during the fourth run of the tape, Bianca had snapped. "Don't you have any more music?"

"What's the matter? You're not a fan?" Michael turned back to look at her, offended.

"I was three hours ago."

Michael ignored her and turned the volume up, singing along this time.

Nancy rolled in her seat once again.

"The people that watch this documentary won't appreciate all the repeated songs on the soundtrack!" The camera turned to the left, focusing on Daniel, who had woken up to yell at Michael.

"They're right." The camera pointed to the back of the passenger seat where Nancy had just woken up.

Nancy: *I was so tired, I probably wouldn't have been awake enough to even agree with them here, but that damn truck just **had** to shake all the time.*

"Alright, fine!" Michael turned down the music and sighed. "We can ride in silence then."

"Finally!" Nancy and Daniel said together.

"Michael, look out!" Nancy yelled, pointing through the windshield at a couple biking up the mountain in their lane.

Michael pulled the steering wheel hard to the left, swerving the truck out of the way while the passengers all screamed, but none louder than Bianca, who was closest to the camera's microphone prior to dropping it.

As it fell to the floor, it caught glimpses of Bianca and Daniel's bodies swinging violently in their seats and providing excellent examples of visible whiplash.

Bianca picked the camera up and recorded through the rear windshield, catching the bikers sitting on the shoulder of the road with their bikes knocked over.

They flipped off the truck while Michael drove away.

The inside of the truck was in complete silence, minus the sounds of everybody trying to catch their breath, for about two minutes. That silence remained until they descended the mountain and a car horn honked behind them.

Bianca pointed the camera through the rear windshield again, and Mitch's all-white van caught up to them, continuing to honk.

Michael honked his horn in return.

Bianca turned to the front of the truck, where Michael pointed out the sign that read "Final gas station: 30 Miles".

"I think Alyssa wants us to pull over. I think that's a good idea." Michael said.

"Yeah, me too," Daniel said.

***

Camera 1

"I'm sick of holding this thing. It's your turn." Bianca said, passing the camera off.

"I need to go pay for stuff. Give it to Nancy." Michael said.

"Fine," Nancy said, reluctance in her voice. She took the camera and filmed herself getting out of the car, then Mitch's van as it pulled up behind them. She proceeded to follow Michael as they walked toward the gas station store.

"Be sure to keep recording. I'm sure something strange will happen at this middle-of-nowhere gas station." Michael said, opening the door to the gas station.

Nancy laughed when Michael gagged upon entering.

Nancy: *It smelled so bad.*

Interviewer: *That bad?*

Nancy: *Like spoiled milk. And the humidity in there was overwhelming. I wish I could say that this was my worst experience of the trip.*

Nancy fixated the camera on the middle-aged white woman working the cash register. She had a displeased expression while working to fix the tiny desk fan in front of her.

Nancy turned the camera toward Bianca and Daniel, who walked through the snack aisle, grabbing enough junk food to satisfy them both for the rest of the week. The footage zoomed in on the occasional hip grab that Daniel would give Bianca while he walked closely behind her.

Nancy: *I'm not sure when their flirting began, but this was the first time I noticed it.*

Interviewer: *That wasn't something you expected?*

Nancy: *What do you mean?*

Interviewer: *When you and Michael invited them? Your two hot, single friends? I feel like it should have been expected for it to happen eventually, with you guys alone in the woods for a long time.*

Nancy: *Well, I didn't **know** that Bianca would've been that attractive when I invited her, and I never really thought of Daniel on that front, either. He was always so stuck up. I guess I just never thought I'd see him make a move on a girl. And sure, I would've maybe expected it deeper into the trip, but this was before we even got there! They hadn't even known each other for a full twenty-four hours yet.*

"Nancy!" Michael's voice could be heard from behind the camera while it kept the focus on Daniel. "Nancy!"

She finally turned the camera toward Michael, who sat impatiently at the cash register.

"Do you want anything else? Snacks? Drinks?" Michael said.

"Yeah, I'll grab a water bottle." She said.

She brought the bottle to the register.

Michael paid for it and a pack of gum that he threw on the counter at the last second. He also added eight dollars to the total for gas.

While the clerk rang him up, Nancy brought the camera to the door, where it sounded like an argument was happening outside.

***

Camera 4

The camera turned on, first pointing at gravel flooring, then to Winston's face.

"Okay, one way or another, I'm finding a different way home." Winston looked back to the van behind him. "The van *reeks* of marijuana. Plus, their air conditioning is broken! And to top it all off...." Winston pressed his palm into his forehead and slid his hand back through his hair. "...They don't even have seats! Lauren and I just sat in the back and rolled around with all of the suitcases and tents! Lauren slammed her head into mine at one point! I have a pretty big head. I didn't even feel it, but I know she did! And don't even get me started on-" There was a vague commotion that could be heard in the background that drew Winston's attention. The camera started to shake while Winston ran toward the scene.

Once it stabilized, it was pointed at Lauren and an older man just outside a gas station building. The man appeared to be somewhere from his early forties to late fifties. He wore an unbuttoned floral shirt and a tattered bucket hat. His dirty attire made him look like he could be homeless, but he had a nice-looking photography camera that hung around his neck. He had a crazy look in his eyes that seemed to protrude from their sockets while he put his finger in Lauren's face, yelling at her.

"You kid's don't even know! You have no idea!" The man brought his attention to Winston and the camera. "You'll die out here! You're all gonna die!"

"What the fuck?" Winston said. "Lauren, who is this?"

She shook her head in what looked like mixed confusion and terror. Her eyes watered.

"You all need to leave! Go back to where you came from! Pack your shit and leave!"

The camera turned to the store's entrance, where Michael and Nancy came rushing out.

"Is everything okay here?" Michael asked,

"No, the hell it isn't!" The old man grabbed Michael by his shoulders while he yelled. "It's not safe out here!"

Michael looked at the camera, confused, and pushed the guy's arms off him. "Winston, who is this guy?"

"I don't know! He keeps telling us that we need to leave!" Winston said.

"I warned you! Don't say I didn't!" The man continued to ramble.

"Can you tell me the problem and make some sense?" Michael said.

"How's this for sense? You're all going to die! You've disturbed her. You've gone and entered her territory. Now he's pissed."

"What? Who did we disturb?" Nancy asked.

"Nancy, don't. He's just some crazy old man. He probably got into Mitch's stash-" Michael said.

"-Who? She asked who? So you don't even know? Ha! And they say I'm the crazy one." The old man said.

Lauren and Nancy exchanged confused looks of worry.

The old man began to laugh before pushing Michael to the ground and running behind the gas station.

"Go after him!" Michael yelled while getting back to his feet.

Winston chased after him, focusing the camera on him as soon as he came into the frame, but he started to descend a steep hill. Winston let the camera follow him until he disappeared into the trees. Once the camera turned around, Michael had finally caught up to Winston.

"Where'd he go?" Michael asked.

"Down there. Sorry, but I wasn't going to follow him into the woods." Winston said.

"Don't worry about it." Michael brushed the gravel off of the back of his pants.

"Are you guys okay?" Nancy asked as she approached with Lauren.

"Yeah, we're fine," Winston said.

"What a fucking asshole," Michael said.

"Oh my God." Lauren looked to Mitch's van, where Alyssa was pumping gas. "Look at all of the smoke coming out of the windows! I think there's a fire inside!"

The camera caught Nancy and Michael cracking a smile when they looked at each other.

"Oh, no!" Nancy said, sarcasm in her voice.

"Quick, go stop it! What if it gets to the gas pump?" Michael said.

Lauren started to run, and the others followed closely behind her, trying not to laugh.

"Alyssa, there's a fire in the van!" Lauren yelled while she ran past her to the back door.

Alyssa continued to pump the gas.

"Be careful. If there's a fire, the door handle might be hot." Michael said.

Without a second thought, Lauren swung the door open, and a cloud of smoke blew straight into Lauren's face as if an industrial-sized fog machine had been running in the van this entire time.

Once the smoke cleared and the camera could focus on the inside of the van, the only fire was coming from Mitch's lighter as he lit another joint.

"Woah, close the door, man! You're letting all the smoke out." Mitch said, laughing.

Nancy: *We were so distracted by Mitch that maybe we forgot about that crazy old man. But we should've listened to him. We had every opportunity this trip to turn around and go home, but we never did. This was just the first example.*

***

Camera 4

This footage began with Winston in the back of Mitch's van. "Alright, it's been maybe an hour since the gas station. We are getting close to our destination, but Mitch couldn't live with himself if he didn't do one last stupid thing before we got there."

Winston's face lit up before he turned the camera to the opened back door of the van.

"Hop in, folks," Mitch said. "Try not to step on anything."

A familiar young couple stepped into the frame and climbed into the back of the van. Their clothes seemed slightly dirty and scratched up, primarily along their knees and elbows. They wore large hiking backpacks that they placed on their laps while they sat crisscrossed on the floor right next to the exit door.

Mitch closed the door behind them.

Nancy: *I'm not surprised that Mitch had picked up hitchhikers, but I am surprised that he managed to find the one pair of hitchhikers that were only hitchhiking **because** Michael almost hit them earlier.*

"Alright, where to?" Alyssa asked while Mitch hopped back into the passenger seat.

"Nowhere specific, we just wanted to go deep into the woods, but our bikes gave out on us a few miles back after some asshole almost hit us." The man said.

Nancy: *I've always felt guilty about this, but I don't think I could've done anything more to avoid it. I suppose I should've made Michael pay more attention to the road.*

"Sounds good to us. We are just going a few miles deeper ourselves. We can part ways when we get there." Alyssa said, putting the van into gear.

"Perfect." The couple said in unison.

Alyssa took off fast enough to shift all the loose bags in the back. Lauren even had to stop Winston's suitcase from rolling into her. "Sorry! We have to catch up to Michael."

Lauren broke the silence. "So ... I'm Lauren, and this is Winston. It's nice to meet you guys." She gave a lighthearted wave and smiled.

"Nice to meet you!" The rough-looking girl spoke with a high-pitched voice that didn't suit her. "I'm Cindy, and this is Tommy."

Tommy seemed annoyed but waved back. "What's with the camera?" He asked, never removing his gaze from the lens.

"We're making a documentary. Looking for Bigfoot." Winston said.

Tommy and Cindy exchanged looks, hers of excitement and his of hilarity.

"It's for a school project," Winston said.

"Oh, that makes sense! I thought you actually believed in that crap." Tommy said, warranting a slap on his knee from Cindy.

"Be nice." She said.

Nancy: *Winston didn't say anything there, but I'm sure he was offended.*

"So, that explains why you guys are out here! How long do you plan on staying?" Cindy asked.

"The plan is one full week," Winston said.

"Wow, that sounds like fun!"

"Hopefully. Worst case scenario, we are just camping with a bunch of friends. I can't see much going wrong." Lauren said.

"What about you guys?" Winston asked, drawing looks of confusion from Tommy and Cindy. "What are you planning on doing all alone in the woods?"

"Oh! We do this all the time. Be it exercise, entertainment, or anything really. Any excuse to escape from the rest of the world, we love it."

"Amen!" Mitch shouted from the front of the van.

"Well, for the sake of the documentary, can I ask you guys your opinion on Bigfoot? Obviously, Tommy doesn't think he's real, but what about you, Cindy?"

"I saw one!" Cindy said.

"Bullshit." Tommy quickly rejected the idea.

Nancy: *Clearly, this is a hot discussion topic for them.*

"It's not bullshit. I did see one!" She said.

"Winston leaned the camera closer to her. "Why don't you tell us about it?"

Interviewer: *Winston has a knack for this whole interviewing thing.*

Nancy: *He's not a man of many talents, but he tends to take things like this seriously.*

"Well, I don't really know what I saw," Cindy said.

"Don't be shy about it now, babe. That cat's out of the bag. And you were so excited to tell this crazy story to *my* friends. Might as well embarrass yourself here, too." Tommy said.

"Okay, fine. We were out on one of our usual excursions. This was early on in Tommy and I's relationship, so it must've been one of the first times we went into the woods together. Tommy went off trail to use the bathroom, and I heard something rustling in the bushes."

The camera slowly zoomed in on Cindy's face.

"I walked off the trail just a bit to see what it was, and then I saw it … or something."

"Well, what was it?" Winston asked.

"I'm not sure. It was some big, hairy creature. I saw its backside while it was bent over, eating some other big animal. I think a deer. It must've heard me step on a twig or something because it turned around so quickly I didn't even have time to look at it. I was so scared. I ran off screaming Tommy's name. When he found me, there was no sign of that thing!"

"So you didn't see its face?"

"No, I didn't! I got out of there so fast. I about jumped out of my skin."

"I went back to where she said it happened, and there wasn't even a deer carcass there. No skeleton or anything. I mean, come on." Tommy chuckled.

Winston zoomed the camera out and pointed it to Tommy.

"We're in California. Even *if* she saw something, it must have been a bear, right?" Tommy looked to Lauren and then Winston, waiting for approval, but it remained silent.

"It wasn't a bear." The camera turned back to Cindy. "I've seen bears. Plenty. This was different."

The horn from Michael's truck could be heard up ahead.

"We're here!" Alyssa said.

Chapter 5

Campfire Stories

Camera 1

Nancy recorded as Michael pulled the truck off the main road, between a man-made dirt path through the trees, and parked in a flat, open area.

"This seems to be as good a place as any," Michael said.

"Yep, looks good to me," Daniel said from the back seat.

They all got out of the car while Nancy filmed Alyssa pulling Mitch's van in slowly behind them. Nancy scanned the vicinity with the camera. Tall trees towered over them from every angle. Beneath her was a dirt floor that had been paved by the hundreds of campers that would pull off-road to this very spot.

Nancy: *Wow.*

Interviewer: *Does this bring back memories.*

Nancy: *Yes. So many. Not all of them good, unfortunately.*

Nancy took a deep breath of the dry California air as she filmed Michael and Daniel grabbing their tents from the truck's bed.

"You ever set one of these up before?" Daniel asked.

"Absolutely not." Michael said. "Nancy put the camera down for a minute. I need your help with this."

"You boys do it!" Bianca finally got out of the truck. She took some time to stretch before she finished her thought. "Nancy and I have some much-needed girl talk to attend to."

Nancy: *I really wasn't in the mood to set up a tent after that road trip. Plus, I was excited to talk to Bianca after all of this time finally. It just wasn't the conversation I thought it was going to be.*

Nancy and Bianca found a circle set up by a previous camper, built of tree trunks that had fallen over, surrounding a dug-out fire pit. Nancy settled the camera on the fire pit and pointed it toward the tree trunk they sat on as if it were a bench.

"So, what's the deal with Daniel?" Bianca asked.

Nancy hurried to gulp her sip of water from the bottle she had finally opened. "What do you mean?"

"I mean, is he a good guy? Is he an asshole? Is he even single?"

"Yes, very single. And, I don't know, really. I honestly just thought he was really boring."

"You think so?" Bianca looked in his direction while he was still setting up a tent with Michael. "He hasn't bored me yet."

"So, what, you've got a thing for him?"

"Maybe I do. We'll see how this trip goes."

"What's that supposed to mean?"

"Well, I know I was supposed to share a tent with you and Michael, but ... Daniel told me that his tent was big enough for the both of us." Bianca said. "If that's okay with you, I was heavily considering it. I didn't want you to be upset if I was ruining any plans."

"No, of course not! You do you. Michael would probably prefer to be alone with me, anyways."

Bianca noticed Lauren walking towards them. "Oh, hey, girl! How was the drive?"

"It was okay, I guess." Lauren looked as though she needed to get something off of her chest.

"Are you okay? Did something happen?" Nancy asked.

"What? No! I just..." She looked embarrassed.

"What?" Bianca asked.

"Did I hear Bianca say she was sharing a tent with Daniel? Does that mean I could take her spot in your tent?"

"Well, yeah, I don't see why not. I mean, did something happen to yours?" Nancy said.

"I didn't even bring one."

Bianca laughed.

"I didn't even think about it! I wasn't planning on coming to begin with. The whole thing was so last minute for me. I was just worried about getting packed and to your house before you left without me."

"If it makes things better," Winston yelled from the van that wasn't too far from them, "I didn't bring a tent either!"

"What?" Michael yelled, dropping a pole from Daniel's tent, having finished setting up his own. "What do you mean you didn't bring one?"

"Lauren didn't *either!*" Winston yelled back.

Lauren cocked her head back as she took was targeted.

Michael and Winston both walked to the fire pit.

"Why would you guys not bring tents? How are you supposed to sleep?" Michael asked.

"I was hoping to sleep in yours," Lauren spoke quietly.

"I'm sorry, but no," Michael said.

"I was going to sleep with you guys, too," Winston said.

"Fuck no. Daniel told me Bianca would be in his tent, so I finally got some alone potential with Nancy. No offense, but you guys are *not* sleeping in my tent. As a matter of fact," Michael looked toward the van. "Mitch! You brought a tent, right?"

Mitch gave a thumbs up from the passenger seat, where he had not moved since they parked.

"You guys can sleep with Mitch."

"Nope!" Lauren and Winston both yelled.

"I don't think you have much say in the matter," Michael said.

Daniel walked over, no longer trying to set his tent up alone. "What's going on here?"

"Winston and Lauren didn't bring tents," Michael said.

"Wait, seriously?" Daniel said.

"Yeah, that means they've got to sleep with you," Michael said.

"No way, man," Daniel said.

"Yeah, that's not gonna happen," Bianca said.

"Come on. You've got the biggest tent. It's only fair." Michael said.

"There won't be any room. I'm setting up a queen-size air mattress in there. There won't be anywhere for them to sleep." Daniel said.

"An air mattress sounds nice," Winston said.

"That wasn't an invite," Daniel said.

"Okay, how about this?" Nancy said. "There's two extra people and three tents in total. Let's draw sticks for it."

"That's about as fair as it gets," Bianca said.

Michael emphasized his frustration with an exaggerated sigh and stretch combo. "Fine. Get Mitch and Alyssa over here. Let's do it."

***

Camera 2

The group had settled around the fire pit, and Bianca turned her camera on. She rested it on her lap while Daniel stood up with three match sticks in his hand.

"Okay, on these match sticks, I wrote three numbers. Number one is my tent, number two is Michael's, and number three is Mitch's." Daniel walked around the group, showing the matches off, even getting them in the camera frame to prove that he wasn't cheating. "Are there any questions?"

Everyone seemed to understand until Michael raised his hand.

"What's your question?" Daniel asked.

"Why can't they sleep outside? Make their own tent out of sticks and leaves?"

The camera caught a few chuckles from the group, but Winston's face seemed annoyed, and Lauren's face seemed scared as if they were actually going to make her do it.

"Are there any *other* questions?" Daniel asked. "No? Alright, then." Daniel laid the matchsticks next to each other, flat on the ground. "I placed them here on the floor, numbers facing the ground. Lauren, grab a stick. No flipping them over, and the first one you touch is yours.

Lauren stood up from her seat. She brushed dirt speckles from the back of her skirt and slowly approached the sticks. She crouched down, holding her knees with her hands while she observed the matches. "This one!" She reached out and grabbed the stick on the far left. "It says...number three."

In the back of the group, Michael mouthed the words, 'thank God.'

"Mitch's tent it is," Daniel said.

Lauren looked at Mitch while he clapped with a lit joint in his hand. "No, absolutely not."

Michael jumped to his feet. "No, you can't change it now!" He yelled, pointing his finger at Mitch. "Fair is fair."

"If they're going to be smoking all week, I can't be around them like that. I've never done that before!"

"You should've thought about that before you forgot to bring a tent on a *camping* trip," Michael said.

Nancy pulled at his shirt to get him to sit down.

"Look, my grandmother died from lung cancer, okay? I'm sorry I forgot my tent, I just won't do it. Can I pick another stick?"

"You can just stay with us," Bianca said behind the camera.

Daniel, Michael, and Lauren all looked at her.

"She can?" Daniel asked.

"Yeah, it won't be the worst thing," Bianca said. "Michael will throw a fit if she pulls his stick, and I don't want her to hear that from him *all* trip. Then she will be in a poor mood and bring the rest of us down. If we're all going to be together for a week, let's at least have a good time."

"You mean it?" Lauren asked.

"Of course I do. Just don't get afraid or scream if you hear things go bump in the night. Right, Daniel?" Bianca said.

"Yeah, right," Daniel said. "But you have to stay off the air mattress. There won't be enough room for all of us."

"That's okay. I did bring a sleeping bag." Lauren said.

"Okay, my turn!" Winston stood from his seat.

"No, you can sleep in Mitch's tent. She already pulled his stick, and Daniel volunteered, so Nancy and I are safe." Michael said.

"But I didn't get to pull a stick. Fair is fair." Winston said.

"Yeah, what if *we* want some alone time, too? Stop worrying about yourself all the time." Alyssa said.

Michael balled his fast and kept quiet.

Lauren placed the match stick back down and picked up the one that had the number one on it. She then reshuffled them and set them back down.

Winston walked over to them, bent over and grabbed the one on the right, and read it. "Number two."

"Fuck!" Michael yelled and got up. "I'm sick of this." He walked away toward the direction of the cars.

Nancy: *I wasn't pleased about it either, but Michael was pissed. It was a little scary, seeing him get so angry like that.*

Interviewer: *Did he always have anger issues?*

Nancy: *Only when he didn't get things that he wanted. He was spoiled growing up.*

"It's gonna get dark soon," Daniel said. "Let's finish setting up. Get all your stuff out of the cars, and let's have fun tonight."

***

Camera 3

The camera turned on and faced at Alyssa's backside while she bent into the small doorway of a green tent resembling a tepee. "Look at that. We're all done before everyone else." Mitch said from behind the camera.

Alyssa backed out of the tent and spoke directly to the camera. "And guess who set it all up by themself?"

"That's my girl," Mitch said, but Alyssa didn't seem amused.

Nancy: *Alyssa was always good about getting stuff done by herself. She couldn't rely on Mitch too much. He wasn't the handiest person.*

Interviewer: *That tent is quite small, too. Where would Winston or Lauren even fit if they had to sleep there?*

Nancy: *I have no idea. To be fair, we didn't know that their tent was so small when we decided to pull sticks. I wouldn't have let them sleep in there, though. There's no way.*

Alyssa walked back into the frame with a thin fur blanket, and she laid it down on the tent floor, just below their two pillows. She crawled into the tent and patted the spot next to her, insisting that Mitch join her.

Interviewer: *Not even a sleeping bag?*

Nancy: *Of course not. They never fail to surprise me.*

Mitch joined her and set the camera in the corner of the tent, facing both of them. Alyssa reached into her bag and pulled out a joint while Mitch supplied the lighter.

"Have you smoked at all this trip?" Mitch asked.

"Not since this morning. But I feel like I can finally relax." She placed the joint between her lips and held it above the lighter. She took three small test puffs before one long exhale. She ran her fingers through her hair, pulled some knots, and laid down.

"You must be tired from all that driving." Mitch began to rub her knee in circular motions. "Thank you."

"Yeah. My feet are killing me, and I have a headache, but I'm just glad we got here safe." She passed it to Mitch.

"Could you imagine if that girl tried to squeeze in here?" Mitch laughed and took a hit.

"Lauren?" Alyssa looked around the tent. "No, I couldn't. I guess we could've said how small our tent was earlier."

The tent started to fill with smoke.

"Well, I wouldn't worry about it." Mitch took another hit and passed it back. "Any idea what the plan is tomorrow?"

"Find Bigfoot?" There was a long silence that led to an uproar of laughter from the both of them. "I don't even know what the plan is *tonight.*"

"Me neither!" They continued to laugh. "Oh, hey...whatever happened to those hitchhikers we picked up earlier? You know, the ones with the bikes?"

Alyssa looked at him like he was a puppy. A dumb but inno-cent puppy. "You...you don't know?"

Mitch shook his head.

Alyssa choked on her inhale. "They left! Like, as soon as we pulled over! You even offered to come to hang out, but they just left. It was like they just wanted to get out of here as soon as they saw Michael's truck."

Nancy: *I wonder why.*

"Really? That's weird." Mitch reached to grab the joint from her hand.

"What's weird is that you don't remember them leaving. You even said goodbye to them!" Alyssa giggled.

Mitch looked down at the joint in his hand as if it had stolen the memory from his head. He took one last puff before tossing it out of the front of the tent. Alyssa leaned in and kissed him while she kept giggling.

Nancy: *It almost feels invasive watching this.*

Interviewer: *How so? They don't do anything inappropriate here.*

Nancy: *I didn't mean that. I meant watching them together, alone like this. I've never seen that intimate side of their relationship before. I always see them together, laughing and just enjoying life, but I never actually looked at them as a real couple before now. They were just hard to take seriously.*

***

Camera 2

"Day one has been a bit of a nightmare," Bianca spoke to the camera. She looked to be alone in a tent while she worked on reapplying her makeup. "Some people didn't bring tents, others are throwing temper tantrums, and now I probably won't get to have any fun with Daniel tonight because I offered to share this wonderful tent with Lauren."

She applied her eyes shadow and reached into her makeup bag for red lipstick. She applied one layer and rubbed her lips together, finishing with a popping sound. "But I guess it can't be helped. Maybe if I'm in the mood, Lauren will have to cover her ears."

Footsteps could be heard from outside the tent.

"Bianca, are you still in there?" The tent unzipped and the flaps came open with an aggressiveness. Daniel poked his head inside.

"What if I was getting dressed?" She asked.

"Then I'd be a lot happier than I am right now. Why would you volunteer our tent to Lauren?" Daniel asked.

"Because I'd rather have *her* in this tent than Winston. After she drew her stick, there would have only been our two left for Winston. For all we know, he could have made the same complaint about the smoke as she did. And by the looks of their tent, I'm glad we volunteered for her because there is no way in hell he would have fit in theirs."

"Well, when you put it like that-"

"-I'm right. I know." She blew him a kiss. "Now get out of here while I finish getting ready."

"Fine, geez." Daniel backed out of the tent, leaving the flaps open.

"At least zip it up!" Bianca yelled. "God, leave it to the girls to do everything around here."

***

Camera 4

When Winston turned the camera on, he was lying flat on his back inside a sleeping bag. A single light hung from the roof and illuminated the tent. "Here I am, the first night in the woods, and I am already regretting it. Apparently, I'm the bad guy for not bringing my own tent, which to their credit, wasn't very bright. Either way, I'm here, I'm annoyed, and I'm uncomfortable." He shook himself around in the sleeping bag. The tent walls shook with him.

"But we are in a nice little spot in the forest. The air smells fresh, we are just off of the road, and I'm sure if Bigfoot is out here, we will find him." Winston sat up and pointed the camera through the mesh window that ran around the top of the tent.

The daylight had faded. Most of the group gathered around a campfire in the pit where they had drawn sticks around before. "As you can see, it's gotten dark already, and they made a fire. Hopefully, everyone will be done with that soon, and we could all get to sleep for a long day of searching tomorrow."

Winston brought the camera down to the tent door, which was unzipping.

Michael poked his head through the door. "Hey dude, Mitch got this campfire started. You should come to hang out with us."

"Maybe in a little bit. I feel like it's warmer in here." Winston said.

"Sounds good. And, I wanted to apologize about before. I shouldn't have been such an asshole."

"Well, thank you. For letting me sleep in here and for apologizing. I won't hold it against you."

"I hope not. And, uh..." Michael looked behind him awkwardly and leaned back in, keeping it quiet. "You've messed with the camera quite a bit by now, right?"

"Yeah, I think so."

"When I bought them, they advertised this night vision feature, but I can't figure it out. Would you know anything about that?"

"Oh, yeah," Winston brought the camera toward Michael, "you just flick this switch here."

The camera rang, converting the footage into a bright, green, and black filter.

"Just like that?" Michael asked.

"Yep, and flick it back...." The camera footage returned to normal. "and it's off."

"Dude, thank you so much," Michael said.

Winston brought the camera back around and caught Michael's shit-eating grin on his face.

"Seriously, come out and enjoy the fire. It'll be fun. And, thank you." Michael exited the tent with a cheerfulness that he hadn't shown all trip.

"That was weird," Winston said.

Nancy: *Michael really just faked an apology to get Winston to show him how to use the night vision feature.*

Interviewer: *You know by now why he wanted to know so bad, right?*

Nancy: *Of course I do.*

***

Camera 2

Bianca had the camera positioned on the floor beside the log she and Daniel used as a bench.

The rest of the group sat on their own benches, divided as usual—Michael with Nancy and Alyssa with Mitch. However, Lauren found herself next to Alyssa. They were all roasting marshmallows and sipping from various beer cans and bottles. The ice chest sat next to Mitch.

Interviewer: *Were you guys even old enough to drink here?*

Nancy: *Underage drinking, while I don't condone it by any means, was rightfully the least of our worries on this trip.*

"So, Nancy and I were really young...." Bianca looked at Nancy while she thought. "Maybe nine years old? We were on one of our families' many camping trips. We were staying at some shitty campsite."

"Definitely the worst we've ever gone to." Nancy shook her head and laughed.

"So I wake up in the middle of the night, it's probably like three in the morning, and I just *have* to pee," Bianca said.

"So she wakes me up," Nancy said.

"So I wake Nancy up. This was the first time we were allowed to share our own tent together. Anyways, I wake Nancy up, and she is pissed."

Nancy is still laughing behind Bianca.

"She is *so* mad at me for waking her up, but I had to pee, and I didn't want to go alone, so I forced her out of bed. This is the first and only campsite we ever went to that didn't have a bathroom, and our parents warned us not to go anywhere near our tents because bears can pick up the scent and mistake it for food-"

Winston interrupted as he arrived, taking his seat on the floor. "Wait! Are we not supposed to pee around here?"

The entirety of the group looked at him dumbfounded.

"But there wouldn't *actually* be any bears out here, right?" He said.

The group continued to stare, stunned.

"You guys are kidding." Winston stood back up from his seat. "Why would you pick a spot that has bears?"

"We're in California." Michael waved his hand around the forestry that surrounded them. "There is no camping without bears."

"So you thought we would find a Sasquatch out here, but a bear would shock you?" Alyssa asked.

Winston thought about it and sat back down.

"Can I finish my story? Please?" Bianca asked. "Where was I?"

"You had to pee," Daniel said.

"Right. So, little Nancy and I crawl out of the tent and wander off into the woods. Like a dog, I'm sniffing around, trying to find the perfect tree to mark my territory. Once I find it, I make

Nancy stand guard. Make sure some rabid animal doesn't come out and attack me while my pants are down. She starts freaking out when the bushes start to shake. I tell her, 'Be quiet. It's just the wind!'"

"This is my favorite part," Nancy added.

"So I have trouble getting started," Bianca said.

"You what?" Winston asked.

"I couldn't start to pee. I was too nervous or scared. Nancy yells at me to get me to hurry up, when all of a sudden," Bianca leans in towards the fire, "BAM!"

Winston, Lauren, and Mitch visibly jumped from the fright. Even Michael moved his head back.

"Some huge, six-foot-tall monster of a deer fucking leaps out from behind my tree and scares the absolute shit out of the both of us."

"More like scared the piss out of us," Nancy said.

"You shut your mouth," Bianca warned.

"No way, you didn't!" Alyssa kicked her feet with excitement.

"She did!" Nancy said.

"Watch it," Bianca said.

"When the deer jumped out, Bianca fell on her ass and started pissing all over the place," Nancy led the group into an uproar of laughter, aside from Bianca who turned red. "She got it all over herself, the tree, probably even the deer!"

"You're lucky I didn't pee on you!" Bianca ripped her marshmallow off her skewer and tried to toss it at Nancy, but it got stuck to her index finger and just fell to the floor, causing more laughter from the group.

"Speaking of piss," Michael said as he stood from the log, "I'm gonna go do that myself."

"Watch out for deer!" Mitch yelled, and more laughter followed.

Michael exited the camera's view.

"So, anyways," Bianca reached for another marshmallow once the crowd settled. "I finish up, the deer runs off into the woods, Nancy stops her ugly cry-laugh, and we make it back to camp. When we get there, we both notice that our tent is shaking. Like someone was moving inside of it. I got my dad out of his tent to check it out. He didn't know what to do. We didn't know if it was a thief, some homeless person, or what. So, we called the park ranger."

"What did they do?" Winston asked.

"They showed up, ran their flashlight through the tent door, and out comes this little bear cub!" Bianca said.

"Only, it didn't feel so little at the time," Nancy said.

"Yeah, this thing was still as big as Nancy and I."

"Did it hurt you guys?" Winston asked. "Where was its mom?"

"It just ran off, back into the woods. We never saw it again." Bianca said.

"Okay, but wait." Winston held up one finger. "Did this happen because you went pee too close to your tent? I thought you said you went far away?"

"No, this happened because Nancy left her chips in our tent."

"We can't leave chips in our tent, *either*?" Winston asked.

"No, dude. Bears are hungry. You can't leave anything in your tent that smells like anything. That includes deodorant, perfume, and soap. Hell, you can't even leave a bottle of water with you. Bears can sniff out *anything*." Daniel said.

"Jesus Christ." Winston stared into the fire.

"You think bears are scary? Wait until I tell you about the Chupacabra." Daniel said.

Bianca chuckled.

"What, you don't believe in the Chupacabra?" He said.

"The what?" Winston asked.

"Yeah, I'm with Winston," Nancy said.

"The Chupacabra," Bianca said while Daniel rolled his eyes.

"So you don't believe in it, and they haven't even *heard* of it." Daniel shook his head in shame.

"So tell us what it is?" Alyssa said.

"El Chupacabra. The goat-sucker. It's a creature of folklore from Latin America." Daniel said.

"It's like the Hispanic Bigfoot," Bianca said.

"Did he say goat sucker?" Mitch asked.

"If it's the Hispanic version of Bigfoot, why would you believe in it? You don't even believe in Bigfoot." Winston said.

"Because El Chupacabra is *real*." Daniel said.

"How would *you* know?" Alyssa said.

Daniel leaned forward. "Because my mom saw it. She was attacked long before I was born."

"Bullshit," Winston said.

"No, it's true. She has scars to show for it."

"What happened?" Winston asked.

"This was when she was in high school. She lived down South in San Diego, just North of the Mexico border. She had a friend whose parents would go out of town every weekend.

They would always go to their house, drink, party, you know ... high school stuff. One weekend, their parents were suspicious about the parties and stayed home. This forced my mom and her friends to find somewhere else to party. They drove out of town, further South, and found a ranch that looked either abandoned or the owners had fallen asleep. They snuck onto the property and into their barn."

"What happened next?" Winston was leaning as forward as he could, the prime example of being at the edge of his seat.

"They partied, got drunk, danced, the usual. Until shortly after, when they started to explore the ranch, all the animals, from the sheep to the cows, even the horses in their stables, were dead. Some animal attacked them. But not just any animal. El Chupacabra. She said their bodies had been completely drained of blood. Their limbs were torn completely off from the rest of their bodies. No regular animal could have done that." Daniel said.

"You said it yourself. The ranch was probably abandoned. The animals could have just died and dried up by the time they arrived. Raccoons could've come back for the remains. No big deal." Nancy scoffed.

"That's what they assumed until they saw it. She said it was the size of a large dog with reptilian-like skin and a long tongue. Longer than its own body. It ran at them, jumping on her friends and tearing them apart. It even caught one of them with its tongue while they tried to run away. She watched it suck their blood while still breathing until they had no light left in their eyes. My mom only got away because she had the keys to the car."

"Sounds to me like she made up a story to convince you not to go drinking in the middle of the night with your friends," Bianca said.

"I'm sure you have plenty of those," Daniel said.

"You have no idea," Bianca said, but she didn't think it was funny.

"He said she has a scar from it, though!" Winston said.

"She does. A big slash on her back. It was on her, but her friend jumped on it to save her. She lost her life."

"Well, please forgive me if I'm wrong, but I don't believe it," Nancy said.

"You don't have to. Nobody ever does. But I know it's true," Daniel said.

"I mean, why not? We are all out here looking for Bigfoot, so why can't this one be real?" Alyssa said.

Nancy: *It's a bit ironic that I wouldn't believe Daniel's story when we were in the middle of our own unbelievable story.*

"Well, if you guys find that hard to believe, you should hear Bianca's story about the Jersey Devil," Nancy said.

Bianca spit out some beer.

"What the hell is that?" Lauren asked.

"Tell them, Bianca," Nancy said.

"I'm sorry, what are you talking about?" Bianca asked

"Oh, don't act like you forgot!" Nancy said.

Bianca's eyes widened.

"In freshman year you told me about it over the phone, remember? You said there was some rumor about a monster near where you lived."

Bianca's eyes relaxed in relief. "Oh, that's right. The Jersey Devil." She laughed nervously.

"Isn't that a hockey team?" Daniel asked.

"Yes, it is. They named the team after the monster, which I assume is about as real as the Chupacabra." Bianca tossed her head back, letting her hair flow back over her right shoulder. "But maybe I'll save that story for another campfire. Besides, shouldn't Michael be back by now? It shouldn't take this long to pee." She wiped the sweat off her forehead.

"He's probably not peeing. Did anyone see him grab a shovel?" Mitch said.

"No, he didn't. I'll go check on him." Nancy said, getting up from her log.

"While she does that, Daniel, why don't you tell us more about this goat sucker?" Mitch asked.

Chapter 6

Things Go Bump in the Night

Camera 1

Michael placed the camera on the ground while he urinated. His backside was the camera's focus while he aimed his stream at a tree, bouncing up and down while he shook at the last few drops. He zipped up his pants and picked the camera back up. "Time to try this out." With a flick and a flash of light, the camera filter turned green, and the night vision setting flickered on.

"It's only a matter of time before Nancy comes looking for me, so I'm gonna play a prank on her. He moved the camera back to the floor and buried it deep beneath a bush. He moved some of the shrubbery out of the frame, and the camera had a clear view of the small area where Michael stood. He kicked his shoes off and tossed them out of the frame. He removed his shirt, threw it to the ground, and dirtied it by stomping it and scraping it along the floor. He even picked up a stick and cut holes into it. He tossed it on the floor nearby. He squatted in front of the bush to speak directly to the camera.

"The plan is for Nancy to question why I've been out here so long and to come looking for me. She's going to find my ruined shirt and my shoes over there. I want her to think some animal attacked me. When she looks at her most frightened, I'm gonna jump out of the bush and scare the shit out of her. I promised you at this documentary's beginning that we would get some ... *extracurricular* footage. Assuming Nancy comes alone, this is the time for it." Michael stood up and kicked off his pants and socks. He leaned over the bush the camera was hiding in, and rustling sounds could be heard while he hid them inside.

Interviewer: *So, what did you think of his little plan?*

Nancy: *It would've been better if it stopped at the scare.*

Interviewer: *Now would be the last chance to tell us not to show this footage.*

Nancy: *You know why we have to.*

"Michael?" Nancy's yelled in the distance.

"Shit, she's coming," Michael said. Dressed in nothing but his underwear, Michael scrambled to the same tree that he had just emptied his bladder on and stepped behind it.

The footage stood still for a few minutes, minus the occasional rustles in the bushes as the sounds of wind picked up and filled the microphone.

With Michael's shoes in her hands, Nancy gasped and jogged into the frame. She bent down to examine the shirt he had laid for her. "Michael?" She yelled out once more, but he kept it quiet. She turned toward the bush opposite the camera as it shook with the wind. "This better not be some sort of joke." She stood back up, t-shirt in hand. "Michael-"

"Got ya!" Michael yelled, jumping back into the frame.

Nancy screamed, but Michael covered her mouth with his hand while he hugged her with the other. She ripped his hand from her mouth and punched at his arm in a non-threatening display. "I hate when you do these things! You scared me half to death."

Once she finally got out of his grip, you could see that Michael had found the time to remove his underwear bottoms while he waited for her to find him.

Nancy laughed when she saw that he was naked. "What are you doing?"

"Not so mad at me now, are you?" He approached her with a grin on his face.

"Nice try." She said, trying to take a step back before he caught her hand. "Of course, I'm still mad. You're an ass-" She stopped short when he grabbed the back of her head and pulled her in to kiss her neck.

He didn't take long before removing her jacket and unbuttoning her pants.

She slipped off the tank top she wore underneath, and one foot at a time, she removed her shoes by stepping on the back of her heel with the other. She slid down her pants to her knees and let them drop to her ankles, but when she tried to step out of them, she slipped, bringing them to the floor. This didn't slow their pace, as Michael rolled on top of her and only took his mouth off hers when she had something to say.

"Are we really going to do this in the dirt like this?" She said in between kisses.

"Winston is in our tent." He slid her panties down her legs. "I can't think of a better place."

"What if they come looking for us? What if they see us?"

"Then we'd better finish quickly."

Nancy pulled off her bra and tossed it away.

Nancy: *For those of you watching at home, I can understand why you might forget that this is a Bigfoot documentary. But, if I could draw your attention away from my boyfriend and me having sex on the floor, the apparent focal point of this shot, I would like you to see what is happening behind us here.*

Just to the right of the tree, where Nancy and Michael continued to explore each other's bodies, was a bush. Just behind the bush stood something. It looked as though it could be nine feet tall compared to how Michael appeared in the frame earlier. It stood still enough in the frame, and the camera was just blurry enough to make it seem as though it could be just about anything, but with the way its eyes glowed in the night vision filter from the camera and with a sudden tilt of its head, it was undoubtedly a living being. A living being that was much larger than the size of any human and much slimmer than any bear of its size could have been.

It watched them until they finished, and as soon as Michael rolled off of Nancy, it turned from the camera and faded from view.

Interviewer: *Well, that was surely* **something**.

Nancy: *It was.*

Interviewer: *The obvious question here is, and forgive me for asking but did you fake it?*

Nancy: *The orgasm, maybe. But not the footage. As I've said, these are all completely untouched tapes, and we've got Bigfoot on camera. Front and center. Yet, people still won't believe me. I not only wish Michael had not only watched the footage, which I'm sure he did, but I wish he had watched it close enough to notice it in the background. Maybe then we would've been smart enough to leave that damn place.*

Interviewer: *I have a few more questions, then. First, did you ever hear anything that might have startled you in those moments?*

Nancy: *I was kind of busy. I couldn't hear much over Michael's incessant breathing.*

Interviewer: *Okay, and what do you have to say to everybody that suggests it was one of your friends in a giant furry suit?*

Nancy: *That thing in the video is **huge**. None of my friends are even close to tall enough to fill a suit that large. It's just not possible.*

Interviewer: *Fair enough. Let's continue.*

***

Camera 4

"Daniel!" Winston yelled with urgency. The camera shook as Winston jogged to Daniel's tent.

"What's up?" Daniel asked, holding the flap of his door open so Winston could see inside.

"Nancy and Michael aren't in the tent. I don't think they ever came back!"

"Really?" Bianca sat up inside the tent. She was behind Daniel, covering her upper torso with the blanket.

"Yeah, we've got to go find them. It's way too dark out here." Winston said.

"Okay, give me a second," Daniel said.

"Hurry it up."

"Yeah, yeah," Daniel said.

"Is everything okay?" A very quiet Lauren asked from inside the tent, invisible to the camera.

"Yeah, just go back to sleep," Bianca said.

Daniel stepped out of the tent wearing just his basketball shorts and a pair of shoes that he had rushed to put on. "Toss me that." He pointed into the tent doorway.

Bianca tossed him the shirt he had worn at the campfire, and he slipped it on.

"Let's go," Winston said.

"I'll be right back," Daniel said, zipping up the tent door before leading into the woods.

Winston followed behind him closely with a flashlight that he pointed around the forest as they walked. "Nancy!"

"Michael!" Daniel yelled. "Are you guys out here?"

The camera picked up the sounds of something scrambling nearby.

"Come on, this way!" Daniel said, waving Winston to follow him while he sprinted between the trees.

"Don't go too fast. I can't see shit out here." Winston said in between heavy breaths. The camera couldn't pick up anything until they stopped. When Winston focused the flashlight on them, Nancy and Michael struggled to get their pants back on.

"Turn the flashlight off, have some decency," Michael said, lifting a hand to block the bright light from blinding himself.

"Were you guys doing it out here?" Daniel said with a big grin on his face. He didn't wait for an answer, as the shame on Nancy's face was enough for anybody to understand what had happened there. "Oh! In the middle of the woods? In the darkness? You guys are nasty!"

"Seriously, Winston, turn off the damn light." Nancy buttoned her pants and picked her tank top up from the ground.

"Right, sorry," Winston said. Before he switched on the night vision, the footage went dark for a brief moment. "We were just worried about you guys. You've been gone a long time."

"It wasn't that long," Nancy said.

"It was long enough," Michael argued. "And obviously, we were busy. We figured you would've gone to bed by now."

"I was going to, but the tent was empty," Winston said.

"Did you need me to tuck you in? Come on, let's go back to camp." Michael said.

"Hey, Michael?" Nancy said, looking into a bush. "What's this?" She pointed to Michael's camera hidden in the bush. Only it wasn't in its original position that Michael had left it before. It was knocked on its side and pointing only deeper into the bush.

"Uhm-" Michael scratched his head.

"At least you had the decency to point it away from us." Nancy picked up the camera and rose to her feet. She handed the camera to Michael.

His posture made it evident that he was confused, but it didn't stop him from taking the credit. "I wasn't gonna record something like that without you knowing about it first."

"Can we go now?" Daniel asked.

"Yeah, let's," Michael said. "Winston, can you take Nancy back to camp? I need Daniel's help real quick."

"Sure." Winston led the way. He remained silent the entire walk back.

***

Camera 1

The camera turned on, but it was clear that Michael wasn't focusing on aiming it at anything in particular. It remained dark while Michael and Daniel spoke.

"Did you guys fuck with my camera?" Michael asked.

"What?" Daniel asked.

"When she found the camera just now, it wasn't pointing the same way I had it when I put it there."

"So you *were* trying to film her?"

"That's not the point. Did you guys knock it over or not?"

"No, we didn't. Honestly, we had just gotten there when we found you. No games or anything."

"Well, *someone* knocked it over."

"Did you hear anything?"

"Just Nancy's screaming."

"I'm being serious."

Nancy: *I don't recall any screaming on that tape.*

"So am I!" Michael said. "Look, I'm freaking out. I mean, if it wasn't you guys, who was it? If some fucking pervert is out here spying on us, we need to know."

"It was probably a raccoon or something. We *are* in the forest. Just relax."

"You're right. Just ... be careful. Keep an eye out, you know? But don't say anything about this to anyone. *Especially* Nancy. She will kill me."

"What are you guys doing? Hurry up!" Nancy yelled in the distance.

"I mean it. She can never know about this. Complete silence."
Michael said.

"My lips are sealed," Daniel said.

Nancy: *So much for me, never knowing about it. The whole world knows now. I'm just glad the tape wasn't **completely** useless.*

***

Camera 2

When Bianca turned the camera on, it was aiming at Lauren. She was asleep in a sleeping bag with a crooked eye mask on her face. She was snoring.

"I already knew Daniel was gonna keep me up all night with his snoring, but apparently, Lauren is even worse." Bianca pointed the camera to herself. She covered her chest with a blanket beneath a dim light that illuminated the tent. She looked past the camera when the sounds of the flap unzipping occurred. "Back already? Are they okay?"

"Yeah-" Daniel spoke, but Bianca shushed him and pointed her eyes toward Lauren. "Yeah, they're okay." He whispered.

"Where were they?"

"Believe it or not, they were doing it in the middle of the forest." Daniel sat on the bed beside her.

"Doing it?" Bianca seemed confused before the look of realization struck her face. "Oh! *Doing it,* doing it?"

"Yeah. And Michael was trying to be sneaky and film the whole thing."

Nancy: *So much for that being a secret.*

"Well, *someone* has to get it in on this trip." Bianca put the camera down just beside the tent entrance.

"What's that supposed to mean?" Daniel asked.

Bianca dropped the blanket, exposing her bare breasts.

Daniel sat bewildered.

Bianca pulled him by the collar into a kiss.

"What about Lauren?" Daniel said.

Lauren's snore volume increased.

"She won't wake up," Bianca said.

They continued to kiss. Daniel got on top of her. "Oh, we forgot to turn the camera off." He reached over for the camera, but she grabbed his arm.

"Why do you think I turned it on in the first place?"

Daniel's eyebrows raised as he went in for more. The blanket on the bed fell off shortly after, covering up the lens.

Nancy: *It wasn't a long film, but at least every party consented.*

***

Camera 3

"Do you hear that?" Mitch asked. The camera sat elevated in their tent, recording the couple, illuminated by the moonlight that shone through the open end of their tent. The camera could hear the sounds of tent fabric shuffling in the distant background.

"Jesus, you're still awake?" Alyssa asked.

"I think so."

Alyssa rolled over beneath her thin blanket on the floor. "It's probably Michael and Nancy."

Mitch sat up and peeked his head out of the tent. "No, it's definitely coming from the next tent over. It's shaking like crazy." He laid back down.

"Gross."

"It must be Lauren and Bianca."

"*What*?" Alyssa burst into laughter.

The tent shuffling went silent.

Mitch waited for it to resume before he continued. "You know. Bianca and Lauren. They must be mating."

"Mating? You couldn't find a better word?"

"Making love?"

"I'm not sure which is worse."

"Sex."

"Yeah, I get that, but what the *hell* makes you think that it was between those two? Wouldn't it make more sense to be Daniel and Bianca?"

"No. He doesn't like colored people."

"What the fuck?" Alyssa laughed, holding onto her stomach. "Bianca is the most pale person in our group!"

"Yeah, but she's Mexican."

"So is he!"

"But his dad's a cop. Plus, he's training to be one. Aren't they all racist? It's like genetic or something."

"I think you smoked a little bit too much today."

Mitch just stared back at her.

"You think it's more likely that the two girls are having sex rather than the two that have been flirting with each other all day?"

"Yeah. Girls are into that sort of stuff."

"What stuff?"

"Girls."

"You think all girls are into girls?"

"Yup."

"So what about me? Do you think *I'm* into girls? After all the stuff we've done?"

"God, I hope so."

"What? Why?"

"Because I know you're into me, and if you're into girls too, let me know. We can figure something out. Make some arrangements." Mitch rolled over.

Alyssa took a second to gather her thoughts while her mouth sat agape, slightly curled at the ends in an entertained smile. "You, fucking-" Alyssa's sentence was cut off by a sudden arrival of Mitch's snoring. She shook her head and closed her eyes.

Daniel's tent went silent shortly after.

Chapter 7

The First Hike

Camera 2

The next piece of footage began pointing directly at Bianca as she held up a watch. "Assuming Daniel's watch is accurate, it is super fucking early right now." Her hair was a mess. It looked like pigeons had built a nest surrounding a vacant beehive. Her eyes seemed doubly tired from a combination of bags that sunk beneath them and makeup smeared from the night before.

She waved the camera around the tent, which was empty and silent, excluding a faint popping sound that seemed to be coming from outside. "I'm alone in my tent right now, I don't know when that happened, and I keep hearing this strange noise outside. Listen." She adjusted the camera so that it was next to the interior tent wall. The popping sounds grew slightly in volume. The sounds could have been anything from the popping of popcorn, the crackling of a campfire, or even leaves rustling in the wind. The camera's poor microphone quality wasn't much help. "For the record, I'm not scared. After I die from checking out this noise, I just figured I want the evidence to be recorded."

Nancy: *Sure.*

She placed the camera on the floor, pointing from her feet to her ankles as she stood up from the air mattress. Her hair flowed down into the frame, along with her forearm, while she picked up a t-shirt from the floor, and once Bianca lifted the camera from the ground again, she was wearing it.

Her hands shivered in the camera frame while she unzipped the tent. She tried to peek through a small hole in the exit, but the disappointment on her face made it clear that she couldn't see where the noise was coming from. She fully opened the tent exit and reached her head out.

"It's about time! And you didn't even brush your hair yet?" Daniel's voice rang into the microphone before she directed the camera at him. He stood over a portable stove top on one of the logs surrounding the campfire.

Seated around the circle was everybody else in the group, minus Winston. They all had paper plates, some filled with pancakes and bacon, while others were awaiting their turn. Alyssa held just a napkin with a handful of bacon inside that she ate with her fingers.

"Who eats breakfast this early? How are you all even awake right now?" Bianca yelled to them.

"Haven't you been camping before? You should know how quickly it gets dark out here." Michael said.

Daniel used a spatula to flip over what looked like a not-just-ready pancake. "We need all the daylight we can get. We've got Bigfoot to find, remember?" Sarcasm emanated from his voice. "Why don't you come out here, and I'll make you something to eat?"

Bianca brought the camera back to herself just in time to see her eyes rolling while she went back into the tent. "They were giving me a headache." She told the camera while she lay on the bed and sat the camera on the opposite end of it, aiming at herself. From this point of view, it is seen that she is not wearing pants. "And the mysterious sounds were just coming from bacon grease. Just the thing I wanted to wake up to." She shook her head and let out a questionable laugh. "Bacon?" She pulled her shirt up to just below her chest and placed her hands on her stomach. "Does it look like I eat bacon?"

Nancy: *No, it really doesn't.*

"Maybe a long time ago." Bianca threw her shirt back down and rolled toward the camera. Her eyes were closed, but they were watery beneath her lashes. "I wish we never moved." She sniffled. "Nancy got to stay here, meet all of these new people, find the perfect boyfriend, and be happy."

Nancy: *What is happening here? I didn't know she felt that way.*

"But *I* had to move to fucking New Jersey and flip my whole life upside down. It's not easy to make new friends, especially with people that grew up on an entirely different coastline. I had to dress differently, work out, diet, and try as hard as I could to get people's attention and make some new friends. At least, that's what I thought. I don't even know who I am anymore. And that's not even to mention what happened after prom. I finally meet some friends that make me feel welcome, and then I lose them all, and we have to move back."

Nancy: *What happened at prom?*

"I'm sorry this is hitting me like it is. I just miss my old life and Michael's right. I *should* know more about camping, and I *don't*. Now, look at me. I'm on a trip with my best friend, and I'm barely even talking to her. It's like I don't know how. I go through one tragedy, and I forget how to be a regular person. I forgot how to have fun. Fuck this." Bianca sat up from the air mattress and started digging for something beside her bed. She pulled out a pair of jeans and a pocket knife and began to carve at the jeans. Once she had finished, she slipped on her new cut-off shorts. Her right leg was cut higher than the left, and they hugged her upper thighs tightly. "I didn't have great camping gear to pack, and those pants wouldn't have let me do *anything* in them. I'm not gonna let that ruin this trip. From now on, I'm having fun and gonna do it right."

"Bianca, are you gonna eat?" Daniel's said from outside the tent.

"Yeah, give me a minute!" She yelled back. "Sorry about the rant. Once I figure out how I will probably erase that footage, but it was nice to get that all out finally."

***

Camera 4

"I smell bacon," Winston said as soon as the footage started. He was seated in his sleeping bag, his hair more of a mess than usual, and dry drool from the night before stained his cheek. He stretched his arms upward, and his stomach fell out of the bottom of his shirt as it lifted while he yawned. "It's the first morning in the woods. I think I heard we were supposed to go hiking today. I guess I'm excited. I've never been hiking before, and it sounds dreadful, but maybe we will see Bigfoot. But for now, I need to find that bacon."

***

Camera 2

Once the camera turned back on, Bianca's hair was long, brushed, and straightened, plus she had fixed her makeup. She wore notably less than before, just a simple eyeliner and lipstick a single shade lighter pink than her natural lips.

She unzipped and stepped out of the tent. It was already brighter outside than before, and Winston had since joined the group.

"Are you finally ready to eat? I made you a plate." Daniel said. "I didn't know what you wanted, so I just gave you a little bit of everything."

"That's fine, thank you." She said.

"She couldn't eat without brushing her hair first," Michael said.

Bianca ignored him. She picked up her plate after Daniel pointed her to it and sat next to Mitch and Alyssa. She set the camera on the floor and pointed it at the three of them. "Did you guys eat?"

"Yeah, I just finished," Alyssa said. "I think Mitch's plate is up next."

Mitch leaned forward and yelled to Daniel, "No bacon for me, dude."

"Are you sure? I make it good, I swear." Daniel said.

"No, thanks. It's rude to eat an animal in its home territory." Mitch spread his arms out wide to highlight mother nature.

"But pigs don't-" Bianca started, but Alyssa tapped her knee and mouthed, "Don't bother."

Bianca had her first mouthful of what looked like scrambled eggs and let out a complimentary moan for the chef. "That's good! Where did you learn to cook like that?"

Daniel stepped into the frame just long enough to hand Mitch his plate. "My dad taught me. Well, I watched him cook. We used to have these home-cooked meals every night. Even when he was working, he would always make sure to prepare dinner for us. I used to love watching him cook because it was the most time I could spend with him outside work."

"Well, if he could cook anywhere near as good as this, I'm sure he was great," Mitch said after shoveling an entire pancake down into his stomach.

"Was?" Bianca said.

"Nobody told you?" Alyssa asked.

"My dad's dead," Daniel said, sitting on the log next to them.

Bianca's eye's widened, and eyebrows dropped like they do when someone hears terrible news. "Oh no, I'm so sorry."

"Don't be."

"What happened? If, you know, you don't mind talking about it?"

"He got sick with cancer. It was about three years ago, now? It all happened fast, but I promised him I would take care of the family. I told him not to worry, and he told me not to be sad. He said I would see him again, and I told him I would make him proud by then. So, I learned how to cook, I joined the police academy, just like him, and I'm working on making him proud. I don't give myself time to be sad about it." He said.

Bianca leaned over and put a hand on his shoulder. "I'm sure he'd be proud of you."

"If he isn't already, these eggs ought to do it," Mitch said.

"Thanks." Daniel rubbed Bianca's hand and stood to his feet. "Once you guys are done eating, get ready. We are hiking as soon as everyone is dressed."

***

Camera 1

The camera flicked on, featuring Michael, Bianca, Daniel, Lauren, and Winston, dressed in various hiking outfits as they walked through the trees.

Michael and Daniel wore similar outfits, blue jeans, and tank tops. It appears to be a hot day, with the sunlight beaming into the camera lens and the beads of sweat dripping down Michael's shoulder blades.

Winston wore cargo pants that hung well over his combat boots and an oversized trench coat.

The men were strapped with large camping backpacks and water bottles in mesh side pockets.

Bianca wore a tank top, her newly cut-off jean shorts, and white running shoes. They were already collecting dirt on the base of them, but the smile on her face says that she doesn't care.

Lauren seemed to be the least prepared with a loose blouse, matching white skirt, and flip-flops. "Is the road going to be this rocky the whole way?" She groaned.

"Look, just because you chose to have your toes out on a hike doesn't mean we have to hear about it the whole way," Michael said.

"I was just asking. Besides, nobody told me *not* to!"

"We shouldn't have had to," Nancy said from behind the camera.

Interviewer: *Why didn't Mitch and Alyssa join you on the hike?*

Nancy: *Mitch volunteered to stay behind and watch over the camp. Alyssa volunteered to stay behind and watch over Mitch.*

Interviewer: *Fair enough.*

The forest looked to be lively in the footage. They captured families of squirrels running up and down the surrounding trees. Some would run right up to Nancy but would scurry away when she tried to get a close-up. The audio of plenty of different birds singing around them filled the microphone. Even a deer popped into the frame briefly, and Nancy zoomed in on Bianca's crotch to see if she was peeing herself again.

Mostly, they hiked aimlessly, minus the occasional stop and search for "Bigfoot tracks," until they heard a stream nearby.

"I bet if we follow that, we'll find a lake!" Daniel suggested. "We could catch some fish for dinner."

"Or find a bear with the same idea," Winston said.

"Perhaps a Sasquatch instead," Daniel said. "Come on!" He jogged downhill toward the sound.

The camera shook in Nancy's hand while they followed. It wasn't long until they found the small stream that led to a vast clearing and a crystal-clear lake inside. Gray and brown pebbles surrounded the lake, and an even larger stream flowed into the lake from the hill opposite where they were in between more forestry.

"Hell yeah!" Michael cheered, and Daniel followed him toward the lake. They ran like children.

"This is awesome!" Lauren said. "I wish Alyssa were here to see this."

"She would love it," Nancy said.

Bianca kicked off her shoes and chased Daniel into the water. They were knee-deep when she caught up to him, and they started splashing each other while laughing hysterically.

"Come on, babe!" Michael yelled while he rolled up his pant leg. "Let's get in!"

"Uhm, you guys?" Winston spoke, facing backward toward the direction they had come.

"I don't want to get my clothes wet!" Nancy yelled, ignoring Winston.

"Then take them off!" Michael pulled his shirt over his head.

Lauren had walked over to the small white dock that extended about twice the distance into the lake from where Bianca and Daniel were splashing. She sat in preparation to dip her feet in the lake when Winston yelled over the sounds of everyone else enjoying themselves.

"You guys!" Winston pointed, and Nancy followed with the camera while everyone went silent. A cloud of black smoke was just above the treeline, blowing up to a visible height.

"That's a fire!" Daniel yelled.

"Isn't that towards our camp?" Lauren asked.

Nancy kept the camera on her friends, that awkwardly trudged through the water.

Michael slipped his shirt back on, Bianca just picked up her shoes and held them, and Daniel was still wearing his underwater.

The guys grabbed their bags that they had left near the water, and they all began to sprint through the woods, not so much retracing their steps as they were looking to the smoke cloud for directions, following it like the three wise men did the star. The camera shook in Nancy's hand too much to make out what was happening until a scream stopped her in her tracks.

Bianca had cut her foot open on a sharp rock, now covered in blood. "Go without me. Make sure our stuff is okay." She said.

"I'm not going to leave you injured in the woods," Nancy said.

"The guys can handle it. Let us help you." Lauren said.

They made the guys leave them behind before Nancy shut the camera off, needing both hands to help Bianca to her feet.

Chapter 8

First Blood

Camera 4

The camera turned on to a campsite flooded with smoke and yelling from multiple parties.

"Where is Mitch?" Michael yelled, running out from behind the cameraman.

"Over here!" Alyssa waved them over from behind her tent.

When they got to him, Mitch waved a small blanket over the fire that covered a ten-foot radius across the grass behind their tents.

"Stop this side before it reaches the trees!" Winston yelled from behind the camera. He ran to the tree side and filmed himself stomping at the fire. He looked up with the camera, and Michael had arrived with another blanket that he waved over the fire with him. Daniel brought more blankets to throw over the fire, and Alyssa helped by dumping water bottles on top of them.

"What the hell happened here?" Michael said once they diminished the fire. "You guys were supposed to be watching the camp!"

"We *were*, man," Mitch said.

"So *what* happened?" Daniel said.

"I don't know. I guess I forgot to put my joint out before tossing it."

"Are you fucking stupid? No, of course, you are. But are you *that* fucking stupid?" Michael asked.

"Hey, don't be mean. At least nobody got hurt." Alyssa stepped in.

"I did," Winston said.

"He could've burned the whole camp down! Or worse, the forest!" Michael said.

"My foot kind of burns," Winston said.

"Nobody cares about your damn foot, dude," Daniel said.

"I'm sure it's better than mine." The camera turned to find Bianca limping in between Lauren and Nancy whole, supporting her around their shoulders. She kept her foot off of the ground. Blood dripped into the leaves below.

"What's going on?" Nancy asked.

"This *airhead* over here tried to set the camp on fire," Michael said, pointing to Mitch.

"It wasn't on purpose," Mitch said.

"I don't care if it was on purpose. It was really, *really* stupid!" Mitch looked around at the burned grass with little energy.

"It wasn't your fault, babe. As you said, it wasn't on purpose." Alyssa reached for his hand, but he turned and walked away. She ran after him.

"You don't have to be such a dick," Daniel said.

"Yeah, that seemed kind of harsh," Nancy said.

"What, so *I'm* the bad guy now? He threw out a lit joint in the fucking forest." Michael said.

"Yeah, but still," Nancy said, walking away to seat Lauren and Bianca at their campfire.

Daniel followed them.

"Really? You guys?" Michael asked, dumbfounded.

"Since they're all gone, would you mind checking out the burns on my foot?" Winston asked Michael.

Michael shook his head no and walked away.

Winston turned the camera off.

***

Camera 1

"Knock knock," Nancy spoke from behind the camera. She peeked the camera through the tent and found Michael lying on the air mattress with his eyes closed.

He opened a single eye to acknowledge her presence.

"It's just me! I thought you might want to do an interview … you know, for the documentary!" She said.

"I'm not really in the mood," Michael said. He opened his eyes but stared at the ceiling of the tent.

"Come on." Nancy crawled beside him in bed and put her hand on his chest. "Not even for me?"

He looked past the camera to Nancy with a face that seemed like he thought she was either stupid or annoying before ignoring her completely and rolling over to face the wall.

"Alright then, can't say I didn't try." She pulled her hand away from him, hopped out of bed, and left the tent.

Nancy: *That wasn't a good feeling. I was disappointed about Mitch being so careless, too, but when Michael was angry, he was **angry**. I didn't deserve to be treated like that, and neither did Mitch.*

Nancy brought the camera to the campfire, where Lauren sat beside Bianca, who was having her foot bandaged by Alyssa.

"How's the boyfriend?" Bianca asked.

"Terrible. It's best if we leave him alone for now. Alyssa, I'm really sorry for how mean he was to Mitch." Nancy said.

"Don't be. He might have been careless, but you weren't the one that was mean to him." Alyssa said.

"How's the foot?" Nancy took a seat at the log next to them.

"Better. I've been through worse. I just need to avoid putting a lot of weight on it. You know, if I can." Bianca said.

"Yeah, no more hiking for you," Lauren said.

"Are you kidding? We will go back to the lake *tomorrow*, and I'll swim in it." Bianca said.

"Are you sure?" Nancy asked.

"Yeah, that might not be too smart. You might get an infection!" Alyssa said.

"It's just another part of camping! I'll live." Bianca said.

Alyssa finished wrapping up Bianca's foot and stood up. "That should work for tonight. I'm not so sure about getting it wet tomorrow, but good luck. I'm gonna go see if Mitch has calmed down." Alyssa said.

***

Camera 3

When Alyssa turned her camera on, Mitch was sitting in his usual criss-cross position on the floor, this time noticeably without blankets as they had all been burned.

"Michael's not outside. Why don't you come hang out?" Alyssa asked.

"What?" Mitch asked, opening his eyes.

"That's why you're in here all alone, right? Because Michael was pissed?"

"Oh, no. I'm just thinking."

Alyssa sat the camera down and sat down in front of Mitch. "What are you thinking about?" She grabbed him by the hands.

"I don't remember smoking before the fire."

"What do you mean?"

"I don't think I smoked anything. If I did, I don't remember." He scratched the back of his neck.

"What are you getting at?"

"If I didn't smoke, I couldn't have started that fire."

Alyssa took a terrified glance at the camera. "Are you sure? It wouldn't be the first time that getting high made you forget something."

"That's the thing! I'm not high. Or at least, I wasn't before I came into the tent. It just doesn't make sense."

Alyssa stood up and grabbed the camera. "Well, don't stress about it for too long. I'm sure the fire was a simple accident."

"I know. I just can't figure out how it happened."

"Either way, we are enjoying nature out here. It would be fun if you joined us."

Mitch smiled, and Alyssa exited the tent.

***

Camera 1

When the camera turned on, the group was sitting around the campfire in the middle of a conversation that left everyone with mixed reactions. Nancy's eyes were wide with shock, Bianca was blushing, Lauren looked uncomfortable, Winston looked excited, Mitch wore a tired smile, Alyssa was laughing, and Daniel was trying to hide anger. The song "Sweet Dreams" by Eurythmics played on a nearby speaker.

"Come on, man. You can't ask her to do that." Daniel said.

"She *said* dare, man! Those are the rules." Mitch said.

"Yeah, but-"

"But what?" Bianca interrupted. "Those *are* the rules, and a dare is a dare." She used both hands to grab the bottom of her shirt and lift it up and over her head. Beneath, she wore a white silk bra with pink trim around the cups. She spun her shirt over her head to imitate a stripper and threw her shirt in Daniel's lap while he sunk into his seat in shame.

Michael cheered from behind the camera while Mitch laughed with a huge grin.

Winston gawked at her with a smile that made him seem proud of himself.

"Sweet dare, Winston!" Mitch said.

"That one makes up for sleeping in my tent," Michael said.

"Really, you guys?" Daniel said.

"What's the big deal?" Bianca asked. "Did you think they were *all* yours already?"

"No, I just- look, it's your turn! Pick someone."

"Okay," Bianca scanned the circle, "Winston."

He looked up from her chest, overly attentive to her words.

"Truth or dare?" Bianca asked.

"This game's stupid!" He said.

"Come on. We've all gotta do it." Alyssa said.

"Yeah, man." Mitch gave him a shoulder pat, a little harder than he probably intended.

"Not gonna do it," Winston said.

"So you can dare me to play the rest of the game without a shirt on, *exposing* myself in front of all of you guys, but you can't play when it's your time to shine?" Bianca said.

"Fine, fine!" Winston said. "Truth. I guess."

"Truth it is!" Bianca looked mischievous, holding her index finger to her chin while she thought of her question. "Out of all of us girls, Lauren, Alyssa, Nancy, and myself, which of us do you prefer?"

"What do you mean?"

"You know what I mean. Which of us is your type?" Bianca said.

"My type?"

Alyssa sighed, "Which of us would you want to *fuck*, Winston."

His complexion did its best to hide the blushing, but it was still visible. "Oh!" He looked at each of them one at a time, Bianca even pushing her cleavage closer together with her inner elbows as she stretched her arms to her knees as he looked at her. "None of you."

His friends gave him disappointed groans, and Bianca let go of her seductive pose.

"Nope, tell the truth!" Daniel said.

"Who says I'm lying?" Winston said.

"What, do you not have a preference?" Nancy asked.

"Or maybe women aren't his type," Bianca said.

"Perhaps *none* of you girls are my type. What if I wouldn't fuck any of you?"

The girls gave separate looks of shock, either puckering their lips, raising their eyebrows, or physically putting their hands up in an exaggerated "don't shoot me" pose.

"Okay then ... Your turn. Pick someone else." Bianca said.

"I told you this game is stupid. Someone else go." Winston stood up and stormed away from the campfire.

"Alyssa, truth or dare?" Mitch cracked open a beer.

Alyssa rolled her eyes.

"Dude, toss me one of those," Michael said.

"Same here," Daniel said.

Mitch started handing out beers to the whole crowd. Lauren was the only one to say no, but Mitch ignored her, opened the can, and placed it in front of her. "Drink it. It'll be good for you."

Lauren looked at the can in front of her like it gave her flashbacks of her parents telling her to finish her vegetables.

Mitch brought his attention back to Alyssa. "Truth or dare?"

Alyssa squinted her eyes while she looked at him as if she were trying to see what he was plotting. "Dare. Do you worst."

"Make out with Bianca." He said without skipping a beat.

Alyssa rolled her eyes and looked at Bianca, and neither of them seemed like they were going to back down.

Alyssa stood and approached Bianca while Mitch leaned over to Daniel and whispered something inaudible to him, causing a fist bump between them.

Alyssa leaned in to kiss Bianca's neck just as the song on the radio changed to "Tainted Love" by Soft Cell, bringing in cheers from all the men still sitting in the circle. Alyssa straddled Bianca's lap and began leaving little kisses in a trail up her neck, leading to a bite on her ear lobe where she whispered into her ear.

Bianca smiled and turned her head, bringing her mouth to Alyssa's and engaging in a make-out session that left Nancy and Lauren paralyzed with confusion and Mitch and Daniel covering their laps while their jaws found a new home on the floor.

"What did I tell you?" Mitch said to Daniel, laughing and overly excited.

"Mitch, you are a genius," Daniel said.

"That makes up for setting the camp on fire," Michael said.

"And what *did* you tell Daniel, exactly?" Alyssa asked.

"The same thing I told you last night. Girls like girls." Mitch said.

"Told you," Alyssa said to Bianca before removing herself from her lap.

Bianca laughed.

"What did you tell her?" Mitch asked.

"That you guys are idiots," Bianca said.

All four girls joined in a burst of contagious laughter.

Alyssa stuck her tongue out at Mitch and winked before sitting next to him. "Lauren, you're up! Truth or dare?"

"Uhmm—"

"Dare! Dare! Dare!" Lauren was interrupted by the men's chanting.

"Okay, fine! Dare." Lauren said.

"Make out with Nancy," Michael said, and Nancy shot the camera a disappointed look.

"No, Alyssa has to come up with the dare!" Lauren said.

"Alyssa, just do this for me," Michael said.

"I'm not gonna make her do that," Alyssa said.

Lauren perked up in her seat.

"Let me think," Alyssa looked around, mainly toward the trees in the distance, "I dare you to run."

"What?" Lauren asked.

The crowd seemed confused and disappointed.

"Run. That way." She pointed her finger into the woods. "Run as fast as you can, straight into the woods. Count to fifty, turn around, and come back.

"That dare is lame," Michael said.

"At least it's original," Alyssa said.

"But what if there's a bear out there?" Lauren asked.

"You better be quick on your way back, then," Bianca said.

"What if I hurt myself? No offense, but I don't want to hurt myself like Bianca for the rest of the trip."

"That's my dare. It's either that or make out with Nancy." Alyssa said.

"I'd rather not," Lauren said.

"The decision is yours," Alyssa said.

"Okay, fine."

"Yes!" All three guys said.

"I'll run," Lauren said.

"Damn." The guys said.

"Would you look at that? I guess all girls *don't* like girls." Alyssa said directly to Mitch.

"Or Nancy's just not her type," Bianca said. "I bet she'd be all for it if it were me."

Lauren rolled her eyes and began stretching. "Are you ready?"

"Are you?" Alyssa asked.

Lauren grabbed her beer and chugged it. Once it was empty, she tossed it into the dirt and ran straight into the woods.

Mitch started counting to fifty out loud. She was out of sight behind the trees when he got to fifteen. Once he got to thirty-three, Lauren began to scream.

***

Camera 3

Alyssa's camera had been rolling through their game of truth or dare. She picked it up and followed closely behind Michael and Daniel as they ran into the woods after Lauren.

When they caught up to her, she was on her knees on the forest floor. It was clear that she had fallen, but that wasn't why she was screaming. It was what she tripped over that was truly terrifying.

She was hysteric, screaming and crying together while she pointed toward the human leg that stuck out of the brush beside her.

"Oh my God," Michael said.

Alyssa leaned in with the camera beside Daniel, who dug into the shrubbery to reveal the two corpses of a young, recognizable couple.

"What the *fuck*?" Daniel yelled, falling back from the sight.

Both corpses were utterly ravaged.

The male's neck was twisted to an almost ninety-degree angle, tearing halfway through from the base, the strength of his spine keeping him from complete decapitation. Blood and dirt stained his entire face. Whatever flesh remained visible was purple with bruising. Bite marks covered his stomach through his shirt. His left arm was removed entirely from the elbow and out of sight.

The female's face was more visible, almost untouched, but her limbs matched the male's neck in that they were bending in directions that God didn't intend them to. She did have one large bite on the left side of her neck, but her most concerning injury was her exposed chest cavity, ribs exposed, broken open, and hollow beneath.

Nancy: *I didn't know they were that bad.*

Interviewer: *What do you mean? You never saw the bodies?*

Nancy: *No, and I'm sure glad I didn't. I think I'm gonna be sick.*

Interviewer: *Do you need anything? Water? Trash can?*

Nancy: *Both. I think I'll be fine, but I'm sure I'll need it later.*

"Oh my God...." Mitch said, sneaking into the camera's view for a peek.

"Lauren, are you okay?" Alyssa brought the camera to her and offered a hand to pick her up.

Lauren stayed on the floor, not seeing the hand. "Are they—? Are they dead?" She stuttered.

"Dead?" The camera swung over to Michael. "They're not just dead."

"Yeah, they're super dead," Mitch said.

Michael looked at him like he was an idiot and shook his head.

"Oh my God." Lauren hyperventilated while she spoke.

Alyssa brought the camera back to her, grabbing her hand and pulling her up without requesting. "Let's get back to camp. We have to do something about this."

"We need to find a park ranger! I mean, look at them!" Daniel said.

Lauren stood on her tiptoes to peek over the bush, only to scream and turn away once she saw them.

"What the *hell* could have done that to them?" Alyssa asked.

"Who knows? We're in a fucking *forest*. Literally, anything could have done this!" Michael said.

"Hey, Alyssa?" Mitch said.

"Is everything okay?" The camera shot back toward the camp, where Nancy was shouting from the entrance to the trees.

"They don't need to see this. Let's go back." Michael said. "Stay over there! We are fine!" Michael started walking back toward the camp with Daniel.

"Alyssa!" Mitch said. He waved his hand, telling Alyssa to bring the camera over to the bodies.

"What?" Alyssa asked.

"Isn't this that couple from the other day? You know, the ones we gave a ride to?"

Alyssa brought the camera back over the bush and focused on their faces.

Nancy: *Okay, Alyssa, you can move the camera away now. Yes, it's them. We don't have to look at them anymore.*

"Shit! It is them." Alyssa brought the camera back to Mitch. "Poor guys."

"Yeah, Tommy and Sydney," Mitch said.

"Cindy! Tommy and Cindy!" Lauren yelled.

"Oh, right," Mitch said. "They were nice."

"Come on. Let's get back to camp and go find help." Alyssa pulled Lauren's arm, and they walked back to camp.

Chapter 9

Deaths Bring Questions

Camera 4

"Why did they make *us* go?" Winston asked.

"Would you rather be back in the camp where the attack happened?" Michael asked.

Winston wedged the camera on the dashboard of Michael's truck. He sat in the passenger seat while Michael drove.

"No, not really." Winston's face turned sour.

"They assumed you would be best at giving the park ranger directions to our camp, and this is *my* car. I wasn't going to let someone else drive it. It wasn't a great idea to trust Mitch and Alyssa with something like this, either. Especially after he almost set our camp on fire." Michael said.

"But aren't you worried about Nancy? She should be here, at least."

"She'll be fine. She's smart and tough. Nothing is going to happen to her.

Nancy: *That's so sweet. We had our problems, but he **did** care about me. That's always reassuring.*

"Besides, who else would I trust with all of my stuff at the campsite?" Michael said.

Nancy: *And then he says something like that.*

"So what's the plan? Bring the park ranger to the campsite, answer some questions, pack our stuff and leave?" Winston asked.

Michael's eyebrows raised. He looked at Winston like he was crazy.

"That car ride was so long. I'm not sure I'm ready for another one tonight. And I am *not* riding in Mitch's van on the way home." Winston said.

"Woah, slow your horses. We aren't going anywhere tonight." Michael said.

"Wait until tomorrow, then? That sounds probably best. Still, it's going to be weird sleeping right next to where that couple-"

"We aren't leaving." Michael interrupted.

Winston's head tilted quickly. "What?"

"We aren't leaving. We've only been out here for two days. We've got to finish the trip."

"Uhm, I don't think-"

"What about the documentary? We haven't seen Bigfoot yet. And I spent all this money on these cameras." Michael pointed toward the camera lens.

"Isn't this bigger than a Bigfoot documentary? It's not safe."

"Sure it is. That couple back there?" Michael pointed his thumb backward, referencing their campsite, "They obviously didn't live this life. Plus, we've got more people. Now that we know something is out there, we will be prepared. Besides..."

Winston just stared straight ahead as if he could not believe his hearing.

"What if..." Michael scratched his nose. "And hear me out on this."

"I'm listening," Winston said. He was leaning forward in his seat, looking away from Michael. He seemed prepared to hear the most heinous sentence he had heard all week, including the rambling from the man at the gas station.

"What if Bigfoot was what got to that couple."

"Come on-"

"I'm serious. It would be great for our footage! Did you see the injuries on them? That shit was crazy. If Bigfoot did it, then he is *real*. And we are out here with him. There's no way we're not going to find him."

"No, I didn't see their bodies, and no, Bigfoot didn't do it. I believe in Bigfoot as much as you, but this just sounds like...." Winston stuttered at his loss for words, "Wishful thinking. And not the good kind. I saw those people when they were *alive*, and I don't want their deaths to be spun into some poor-taste money-making scheme."

Michael negatively shook his head while he drove. His tongue flicked around the inside of his closed mouth while he licked his inner gums. "I thought *you*, of all people, would see the potential here. I mean, this documentary was for *you*, anyways."

"Was it? I was fine with writing an essay at home! Camping sounded fun, I guess. At least until I realized I wouldn't sleep in my bed for a week. And now somebody's *dead*. I didn't sign up for that."

"They would've died, regardless of whether or not we showed up."

"Even that's debatable."

"What do you mean?"

"You recognized them, didn't you?"

"What? No?"

"Mitch told me who they were. A couple of bikers. We picked them up yesterday on the way to camp. They mentioned their bikes breaking down after an asshole almost hit them."

"What are you getting at?"

"I overheard you mention the bikers you almost hit to Nancy last night when we were all getting ready to sleep."

"What, so you're saying it's my fault they're dead?"

"No, but at the very least, it is our group's fault that they were out here."

Michael thought for a second. "Who knows about this?"

"Just those of us that rode in the van. I never told anyone else that you almost hit them."

"Good. Keep that between us." Michael looked at Winston. "I mean it. Not a word. And we need to delete this conversation from the camera."

"Seriously?"

"Yes. Seriously. If there is an investigation, fingers might point our way. I don't want them to dig too deep."

"I think it's pretty obvious that an animal did this."

"No. It's obvious that animals got to them. I wouldn't say the initial cause of death would be so obvious."

"I don't think-"

"Can I trust you? If they mention confiscating these cameras, delete this instantly."

Winston nodded.

"You should cut the tape off now while you're at it. We're almost there. I don't want them seeing our cameras before they have to."

Winston reached for the camera, and the footage shut off.

Nancy: *I never knew they had a conversation like this. It answers a lot of questions, honestly.*

Interviewer: *Does it surprise you?*

Nancy: *No, not really. It pisses me off. Everything that happened was avoidable, but we just did everything wrong. I'm proud of Winston for saying something, but Michael's just **so** thick-headed.*

***

Camera 2

The group sat around the unlit campfire again. They had propped up the camera on the log beside Bianca, whose shirt was back on. It was clear that everyone seemed uncomfortable and was making awkward, quick looks toward the woods.

Mitch had "Another One Bites the Dust" by Queen playing on his radio.

Daniel was cooking what looked like cheeseburgers on his stove top, but nobody touched the food he had plated for them.

Nancy: *I remember this! It was such an uncomfortable time for all of us. The air around the camp felt thin. If the fire wasn't enough to scare us, this sure did it. The last thing I wanted to do was eat, but I think that cooking was Daniel's way of coping with the stress.*

Interviewer: *Isn't Mitch's choice of song a little insensitive?*

Nancy: *I doubt it was on purpose. He's an idiot.*

Interviewer: *Fair.*

Daniel put the last burger onto his plate, only recognizing that nobody else had touched theirs afterward. He looked to think about whether or not he could stomach the food and placed his plate on the floor beneath his feet once he took a seat next to Bianca.

"No offense, but I don't know if I can eat anything right now," Bianca said quietly to Daniel.

"Yeah, I get it. The thought of two *bodies* less than sixty yards from us isn't great on the appetite." He said.

"Don't say it like that. It sounds ... insensitive." Lauren said.

"How else would you like me to say it?"

"I don't know. They just deserved better. They were nice people." Lauren said.

"Well, *she* was, maybe," Alyssa said.

Nancy, Daniel, and Bianca shared confused looks.

"You're saying that like you knew them," Daniel said.

"We kind of did," Mitch said.

"What, they didn't tell you?" Lauren said.

The three who were confused only seemed to grow more so.

"Yesterday, on the way in, they were hitchhiking. Mitch thought picking them up would be a good idea, so we gave them a ride out here." Lauren said.

"Really?" Nancy asked.

"We didn't even see them!" Bianca said.

"What were they doing out here?" Daniel asked.

"They left as soon as we pulled in. I barely had a chance to say goodbye." Lauren said.

Daniel's looks of confusion switched to one of suspicion.

"They said they hike out into the woods all the time. They like the freedom of it from the rest of the world." Lauren said.

"If they like hiking, why did they hitch a ride from you guys?" Daniel asked.

"They said someone almost hit them on their bikes, and they broke down," Alyssa said.

Nancy and Bianca looked guilty, but Daniel only grew more suspicious.

"Oh my God," Nancy said.

"No way!" Bianca said, almost excited.

"It was them?" Daniel said.

"What do you mean?" Lauren said.

The three of them looked at each other before answering.

"That was us," Nancy said.

"Well, it was Michael," Daniel said.

"Really?" Alyssa said.

"I feel like that just makes it worse!" Lauren said.

"What? How?" Bianca said.

"If it weren't for us coming out here, they would still be alive!" Lauren said.

"Hey, that's not true," Nancy said.

Alyssa put her hand on Lauren's back. "Yeah, what happened to them? We can't put that on anybody. You can't put that kind of stress on yourself."

Lauren fought back the tears. "Yeah, I guess you're right." She stood up and adjusted her skirt, only to sit back down again. "Look, can we just talk about something else?"

"Just try not to think about it," Alyssa said.

"It's kind of hard not to. We need some distraction." Bianca said.

"Not another game of truth or dare, please," Lauren said.

"I can think of something," Mitch said, pulling a joint from his shirt pocket.

"Do you ever *not* smoke?" Daniel asked.

"Maybe you should try it. It might calm your nerves." Mitch lit it and inhaled.

"Don't be rude. Pass it here!" Bianca held her arm out.

Mitch coughed up his smoke and passed it to her. "You smoke?"

"Duh." She took it from his hand and held it to her lips. She took three small puffs and exhaled it all through her nose at once.

Daniel looked disgusted.

Bianca offered it to him, but he declined, so she passed it to Alyssa instead.

"Is ... is that true?" Lauren asked.

"Is what true?" Alyssa exhaled.

"Does it really calm your nerves?"

Mitch grabbed it from Alyssa and held it out for Lauren. "Only one way to find out."

"It might make someone like *her* freak out, though," Daniel said.

"What's that supposed to mean? Someone like me?" Lauren asked.

"You're just-" Bianca interrupted Daniel.

"A good girl."

"I am not!" Lauren blushed.

"You totally are." Mitch reeled in the joint and took a hit to avoid wasting it.

"How so? Is that what you guys think of me?" Lauren said.

"We can start with how you dress," Daniel said, pointing at her shirt.

"What's wrong with that?"

"It's always skirts and blouses with you. You are always dressing *so* professionally. Maybe you should wear something a little more sleazy. Something *tight*. Show off your ass!" Bianca said.

"Show it off?" Lauren looked confused.

"Yeah, girl!" Nancy said.

"I know you've got a little something under there. I saw it in the little sleep shorts you wore last night. I'd say it's worth showing off." Bianca said.

"I don't want people to get the wrong idea about me. I'm not the sleazy type. I want to save myself for somebody special." Lauren said.

"See? A good girl." Daniel said.

"You can dress sleazy and not sleep around. It's all about making guys think they could have you." Bianca said.

"Come on, guys, you're gonna corrupt the poor girl," Alyssa said.

"I am not some child that you guys can corrupt! I am a grown woman that can make her own decisions." Lauren said.

"And you decide to be a good girl. That's fine. Nobody said it was a bad thing." Daniel said.

"I am not!"

"You wouldn't even sleep in our tent because of the weed smoking," Mitch said.

"To be fair, I wouldn't have been able to fit in that tent."

"But you didn't know that at the time," Daniel said.

Mitch leaned in once again, passing the joint to Lauren. "Feel free to prove us wrong."

Lauren stared at the joint in awe, as if it were her first time seeing a naked man. She reached for it and held it to her eyes, inspecting it as a cop would with a small piece of evidence.

"Hurry up. You're gonna let it burn out!" Mitch said.

Nancy: *The peer pressure was horrible. I want to think I didn't contribute to that, but I certainly didn't help. I was just curious as to whether or not she would.*

Without giving herself time to hesitate, she brought it to her lips and took a long inhale as if she were waiting for someone to tell her to stop. Once she couldn't take anymore, she broke into a coughing fit.

"Shit, are you okay?" Alyssa pats her on the back to help her get it all out.

"I'll-" She wiped the saliva that dripped from her mouth and spat out some more. "-I'll be fine."

"Why'd you take such a big hit?" Bianca asked.

"I didn't know!" Lauren said.

"It's okay. Everyone chokes on their first try." Mitch said before turning to Daniel. "Your turn."

"No. No way." Daniel said.

"Oh, come on," Lauren said.

"After all that pressure on Lauren, you turn out to be a wuss?" Bianca asked.

"That stuff will get me kicked out of the police academy. Try all you want. I am *not* gonna smoke that." Daniel said.

"Oh well," Mitch took the joint from Lauren and took a puff, "more for me, then."

Lauren spat some more and reached out to Mitch for another hit.

"Oh! Look at that! She likes it. Maybe she's not such a good girl after all." Mitch said.

In the distance, the sounds of police *and* ambulance sirens picked up.

"Shit, put that out!" Daniel said.

Alyssa smacked the joint out of Mitch's hand and squished it into the dirt while the rest scrambled to wave away the smoke in the air.

Mitch picked it up and dropped it back into his shirt pocket.

"Make sure it's out this time." Daniel pointed in Mitch's face just as Michael's truck pulled into the campsite.

Bianca picked up the camera and aimed it at the truck that pulled in behind him. The driver-side door had "Park Ranger" painted onto it below an emblem of a mountain range. Just behind them, and with much more urgency, a single police car, followed by an ambulance, rolled in.

Michael and Winston hopped out of the truck. Winston walked toward the group around the fire pit, and Michael met with the ranger at his truck.

"They're this way!" Michael yelled toward the police, that sat in their car with the window rolled down and pointed toward where they found the bodies.

The cop nodded and tipped his hat before hopping out of the car.

The park ranger followed Michael into the woods.

Two paramedics hopped out of the ambulance, one of them grabbed a duffel bag from the back, and they ran into the woods behind Michael.

"Did you guys have a campfire?" Winston asked, his eyes focused on the smoke they failed to clear.

"You can say that." Bianca sat the camera back down, right where it was previously.

"What do we do?" Nancy asked, her body turned completely around to watch the paramedics running through the trees. "Should we help?"

"I don't think there's anything we can do," Daniel said. "Let them work. If they need something, they'll ask for it."

Lauren waved to the cop as he acknowledged them before stepping into the woods. He looked intently around as he walked.

"What do you think he's looking for?" Mitch asked.

"Evidence," Daniel said.

"Maybe the animal that killed them," Winston said.

"He's just checking the scene. I wouldn't worry." Daniel said.

"I just don't think it's safe out here," Winston said.

"Seriously? What, are you scared?" Bianca asked.

"Yes, I am scared. You should all be, too. Those people *died*. Like, super close to where we plan on sleeping tonight." Winston said.

"We'll be fine. Whatever happened to them was just a tragic accident. These things happen," Daniel said.

Nancy looked nervous, biting her nails as she watched the officer.

"I know *I'm* not stressed," Mitch said. "I've got just the thing to calm you down." Mitch started to reach into his pocket, but Alyssa swatted his hand.

"There's a cop here, remember?" She said.

"Oh, right," Mitch said.

"Am I crazy? Am I the only person taking this seriously?" Winston looked to Lauren, whose head was staring straight down toward her lap. "Lauren, help me out here."

Alyssa turned to her and pulled her hair out of her face.

Lauren's eyes were closed. She had fallen asleep.

"Is she okay?" Winston asked.

"Oh, don't worry about her, man. She'll be fine." Mitch giggled.

Nancy: *Maybe if Lauren was awake, she could have talked some sense into us. Ignoring Winston is my biggest regret to this day. I had my concerns, but I didn't want to be the only one agreeing with him. It turns out he was right.*

"What's with the camera?"

Most of the group jumped at the sound of his voice.

Bianca grabbed the camera and aimed it at the cop that approached them from behind. "We're making a documentary."

"It's for a school project," Daniel added.

"Is that right? What's the topic?" The cop sat next to Lauren, who was awake but silent.

"Bigfoot," Winston said, his voice in a higher pitch than usual.

"And that brought you out here?"

"It seemed like a good place to start."

"Well, that scene back there was pretty gruesome." The cop said, gesturing towards the bodies where Michael still talked with the paramedics and park ranger. "Maybe you kids were onto something."

"Really?" Winston asked.

"No. Of course not. My guess is a bear got to them. Little animals got to the aftermath, though I am concerned that you guys didn't hear anything going on."

"We were out hiking this morning. That's probably when it happened."

"Oh, I'm sure." The cop took his hat off and sat it on his lap. "Did you kids know those poor folks?"

"Not really. We just had a small encounter with them." Winston said.

"Yeah? And what was that?"

"We gave them a ride out here. They were hitchhiking a few miles back." Alyssa said.

"Did they say what their business was out here?"

"Just hiking. Nothing more than that." Alyssa said.

"Did they say their names?"

"Yeah, Tommy and Sydney," Mitch said confidently.

"Cindy. Tommy and Cindy." Alyssa said.

"Alright." The cop stood up and turned around. Bianca's injured foot drew his attention. "What happened there?"

"I cut it in the woods," Bianca said.

"You were barefoot in the woods?"

"We went swimming in the lake. Not something I usually do with shoes on."

"Okay, well, maybe ask one of those paramedics out there to look at it. Otherwise, keep it clean. And you kids stay safe out here, you hear?"

"*Is it* safe out here?" Winston asked.

"What do you mean?"

"I mean do you think it's safe here? Or should we pack our stuff and go?"

"You kids will be fine. Just don't go into the woods alone unless you have to shit. Then, at least bring a shovel. Not only to clean up, but it would make a nice weapon. If you see a black bear, yell at it. They're afraid of noise. Nothing else should bother you."

"But, what about them?" Winston pointed towards the corpses. "Something bothered them."

"Bad luck. Who knows? Maybe it was Bigfoot. But seriously, if you kids need anything, please run right back to the ranger station."

Winston pouted.

"Yes, sir," Mitch said, saluting the officer.

The officer glanced at him like an idiot before walking back toward the park ranger at the bodies, passing Michael along the way.

"What did he want?" Michael asked.

"Not much, just a few questions," Daniel said.

Michael was visibly stressed. A bead of sweat ran down his forehead.

"Are you okay, babe?" Nancy asked.

"Yeah, I'm fine." He wiped his forehead and rubbed the sweat onto his pants. "It's just a long day, and it's hot out here." Michael walked past them, and Bianca followed him with the camera until he entered his tent.

Nancy: *Stupid cop. He should've taken this more seriously. Less people would have gotten hurt if he did.*

Chapter 10

Long Night

Camera 1

Nancy had set the camera up at the fire pit that now contained an active fire, and the entire group sat around the fire together. It was starting to get dark. This time around, the group didn't seem to enjoy themselves as much as the night before. It was as if the same animal that tore apart Tommy and Cindy had also ripped the life out of the group.

"Well, if nobody else is hungry." Winston stood up and grabbed one of the cheeseburgers that had gone untouched during the hours since Daniel cooked them.

"How are you even hungry right now?"

"How are you not? We haven't eaten since this morning. I get not having an appetite, but that's got to give at some point." Winston said.

"Yeah, I agree with Winston." Lauren stood up from her seat and grabbed a plate.

"Woah, look who's got the munchies," Daniel said.

"Ha ha." Lauren gave a fake laugh.

"No, they're right. We should all eat." Nancy said, stepping up from her seat on the log. "Should I grab you a plate?" She asked Michael.

"I guess," Michael said. "Thank you."

"I hope the burgers are still good. I'd make more, but I only brought so much food for the trip." Daniel said. "But please, everybody, eat up. We've got another hike tomorrow."

Winston spat out the soda he grabbed from the ice chest beside Mitch. "We do?"

"Where are we going this time?" Bianca asked. "I'm not so sure my foot can handle it." She raised her leg and wiggled her foot that still bled through her bandage.

"Back to the lake," Daniel said. "We need to get our minds off of what happened today. All of us are going, and we are going to have some fun."

"I don't know if I'm really in the mood," Lauren said.

"That." Daniel pointed to her. "That's my point exactly!" He got up and grabbed a plate. "We are in the middle of the woods, and we are all in a shitty mood. Tomorrow, we are going to the lake, and we are fixing it."

"Yeah, he's probably right," Michael said.

"I still think it's a bad idea to stay here in the first place," Winston said.

"I think I could go for a dip. It might make my foot feel better. Bianca said, stretching her leg out.

"Or worse," Winston said.

"Wait!" Alyssa said. "If we all go to the lake, who will watch the camp?"

"I don't think we need to," Michael said. "The drive from here to the ranger station is *so* far away. There's nothing for miles. I doubt somebody will show up while we are gone. Besides, the place is probably in more danger *with* Mitch here."

The group laughed, but Michael seemed serious.

"So what do you guys say?" Daniel asked.

The crowd all agreed. It was like the thought of swimming restored their energy already.

"Then let's finish up here and make for an early sleep. The earlier we get up, the better."

The crowd booed, but they did just that. Once they had eaten their food, they all prepared for bed.

***

Camera 2

"Hey, Michael. Can you come here for a minute?" Daniel said.

The camera only showed the dirt floor, with occasional glimpses of Michael, but it seemed as though Daniel didn't know it was turned on.

"Yeah, what's up?" Michael said.

"You know that couple? The dead ones?"

"Yeah. What about them?"

"Don't you think it was a little weird how they vanished when Mitch dropped them off?"

"Uh, I don't know what you mean. Dropped them off?" Michael sounded nervous.

"Oh, you didn't hear yet?"

"No! What are you talking about?"

Daniel paused briefly. "Mitch gave them a ride out here. After you almost hit them with your truck."

"What?"

"Don't act like you don't remember. I was in the car when you almost hit them! Those bikers yesterday? Remember?"

"Bikers ... bikers ... oh, that's right? What, you're saying those two were the ones that died?"

"Dude, yes!"

"Oh, goodness. I had no idea."

"Yeah, and apparently when they brought them here, they just left without saying anything. I think that's a little suspicious."

"What's suspicious about it? They probably recognized my truck and just left."

"Maybe you're right."

"What did you think happened?"

"What if they wanted revenge? What if they started the fire this morning?"

"Oh shit, you might be right! They were really close to our camp, and I can see why they would be mad. If it *was* them, maybe I was a bit too harsh to Mitch. But I guess we don't need to worry about it anymore since they're dead."

"True. I'm just glad our whole campsite didn't burn down.

***

Camera 4

"Well, today sucked," Winston said to the camera. He sat upright in Michael and Nancy's tent.

Michael and Nancy were asleep on the air mattress behind him.

"We didn't see any signs of Bigfoot on our hike, the idiot stoners almost burned our camp down, Bianca almost lost her foot, I pissed all of the girls off during truth or dare, and on top of all of that, two people died." He looked back at Michael. "This one thinks it's a smart idea to stay here still, and I don't have a ride home, so I'm stuck. This whole trip has been a disaster. I guess we are going back to the lake tomorrow, hopefully, we will find *something* out there, but I'm sure they just want to go and have fun. I guess I understand it, though. What we went through today, maybe we deserve a break—especially poor Lauren. I can't imagine how she felt, tripping over a dead body like that. Still, that's all just more reason for me to want to get out of here."

Winston took a bite of a cheeseburger that looked like he hid in his sleeping bag before reaching back and turning the lamp off. "Day two of the trip is over. See you tomorrow."

***

Camera 2

The camera focused on Lauren inside Daniel's tent. She was pulling all her clothes out of her bag and digging through them on the floor.

"First, you forgot a tent, now tell me … what else did you forget?" Bianca spoke from behind the camera.

"My fucking bathing suit!" Lauren said.

"Woah, potty mouth," Bianca said.

Without looking back, Lauren held a middle finger at the camera

The camera panned to Daniel, who sat beside Bianca on the air mattress. "Good girl gone bad, right?"

"Very funny," Lauren said.

"Why don't you ask Bianca? I'm sure she might have an extra bathing suit. It might be a little small for you, but that shouldn't be a problem. It would probably look better that way." Daniel said.

Bianca shoved him by the shoulder.

"Well, did you bring an extra?" Lauren asked her and plopped down on her pile of clothes.

"To be honest, I wasn't planning on wearing one," Bianca said.

Lauren's jaw dropped in disgust, and Daniel looked dumbfounded.

"Sounds like a party!" Daniel said, jumping on top of her.

"Gross!" Lauren said.

Bianca dropped to the floor.

The footage focused on Lauren while Bianca and Daniel screamed and laughed atop the air mattress while it shook in the camera frame.

"Get a room, you two!" Lauren said.

"This *is* my room! You go get one!" Daniel said.

"Ow, watch my foot!" Bianca said.

"Are you okay?" Daniel asked.

"Yeah, I'm fine.

She didn't seem to notice, but the tent's wall just behind Lauren was slightly pushed in by something roughly the size of two fists. It wasn't until it pulled away, making a loud swiping noise, that she turned around.

"Did you guys hear that?" Lauren said.

"You're still here?" Daniel asked.

"Seriously, I think something is outside our tent," Lauren said.

The camera picked up the sound of an animal sniffing. They didn't seem to hear it.

"Bullshit. It's probably just Winston trying to spy on us." Daniel said.

Leaves crunched outside. They heard it this time.

Bianca grabbed the camera. "I heard it that time."

"What the hell was that?" Lauren asked.

"Let me check." Daniel grabbed the flashlight on his side of the air mattress and unzipped the tent door. He peeked his head out of the tent and flashed the light around the area. "I don't see anything."

Lauren's head jolted toward Bianca, and she screamed.

Bianca followed up with a scream of her own, and the camera started to shake once she jumped away from where she was sitting. Once the footage focused, something was clearly pushing into the tent wall, just behind where Bianca was sitting previously.

Daniel jumped out of the tent and yelled. "Get out of here!"

A large animal roared.

Bianca pointed the camera out of the tent door at Daniel just as he banged the flashlight on the portable stove he left outside the tent.

She didn't catch the animal on camera, but its footsteps were loud as it galloped away.

"Are you guys okay?" Michael yelled outside of the camera's view.

Bianca kept the camera on Daniel.

"Yeah, it was just a black bear. It ran away. Everything's fine. Go back to sleep."

"Are you sure it wasn't Bigfoot?" Mitch yelled from his tent.

"If I didn't think I was gonna piss myself, I would laugh at that," Bianca said.

"Please, no peeing in my tent." Daniel climbed back into the tent and lifted Bianca off the ground, dropping her on the bed.

She screamed.

"Now, where were we?" Daniel said.

"There's something about almost being mauled by a bear that gets you out of the mood, you know?" Bianca said.

"But wouldn't watching me scare it away turn you on?"

"Maybe a little, but Lauren watching us in the corner kind of erases that."

"I guess I'll wait until she falls asleep."

"To be honest, I don't think I'll be doing much sleeping with that bear out there," Lauren said.

"Sounds to me like you're out of luck," Bianca said.

Daniel frowned into the camera before she turned it off.

Chapter 11

Skinny Dipping

Camera 4

The camera flickered on, and Winston's face came into view, yawning and stretching. "Alright, day three in the woods. We're almost halfway through, and there is zero proof of Bigfoot's existence. I'm just hoping someone else speaks some sense to Michael so we can all go home early. I guess we are going to go swimming at the lake today." He shook his head. "If we keep goofing off like this, we will never find Bigfoot."

Winston filmed himself putting on the same cargo pants and the same trench coat that he wore the day before. He grabbed the camera and left the tent.

The group was sitting around the campsite as usual. They all looked tired, except for Daniel.

"What, no breakfast today?" Winston asked. He pointed the camera to Bianca, who was trying her best not to fall asleep on the log that she lay on by herself. "Jesus, you look *awful*. Did you forget to sleep last night?"

"Are you just *completely* unaware of what happened last night?" Daniel asked.

"What, that dead couple? Of course, I'm aware!"

"No, not them. The bear!"

"Bear?"

The whole group groaned.

"Yeah, man. A bear attacked their tent last night." Mitch said.

"No way! Are you guys okay?" He turned the camera to Lauren.

"We're fine. I mean, we aren't hurt or anything." She said. "He was just hungry. Daniel thinks he smelled our burgers from last night."

"Really? So that's why you didn't make breakfast?"

"No shit," Daniel said.

"Does that mean we can't eat in the camp anymore?"

"Not when we plan on leaving our camp unattended in ten minutes," Daniel said.

"So ... no breakfast then?"

Bianca laughed so hard that she choked and rolled off the log.

Alyssa went to her and helped her up. The camera couldn't hear it, but Bianca muttered something to her.

"Let's go, you guys." Daniel tightened the backpack that he wore and grabbed his camera. He walked past Winston, placing a hand on his shoulder. "Sorry, no breakfast."

***

Camera 3

The camera pointed to Mitch's bare feet as the group walked through the woods.

"You could've at least put some shoes on," Alyssa spoke from behind the camera. "Seriously, that's how Bianca got hurt."

"Trust me. It isn't fun." Bianca said.

Alyssa brought the camera up to head height.

Bianca was limping with one arm around Daniel's shoulder.

"We're in nature, baby! If our ancestors didn't wear shoes in the woods, neither will I." Mitch said with his infamous smile on his face. "As long as I don't step on any rocks, I'll be fine- Ow, fuck!" Mitch stopped in place and analyzed the bottom of his foot.

"Are you okay?" Alyssa asked.

"I stepped on a rock."

"That's what you get," Bianca said, laughing.

"It's just a bruise. I'll be okay." He put his foot down and continued on. "You know, I can't help but notice you two getting *real* close on this trip. What's up with that? Are you two, like a thing or something?"

Nancy: *We were all surprised that Mitch could make an actual observation like that.*

"We're just having fun," Daniel said.

"That's what *you* think, but she's digging you, dude. You might want to lock that in." Mitch said.

"No, he's right. It's like when you go to a summer camp and have a seasonal boyfriend you never hear from again. That's pretty much what this is." Bianca said.

"So I won't hear from you again once we get home?" Daniel asked.

"Not unless you earn it."

"Damn, so she's the one using you? That's harsh." Mitch said.

"I'm not *using* him. He's my camp boyfriend. Fun for the week, no strings attached. Back to our normal business operations when we leave here." Bianca said.

"Hell yeah, dude!" Mitch fist-bumped Daniel, who accepted reluctantly.

"So, how's it going so far?" Nancy asked.

"Good for me. I have someone to cater to my injuries. Plus, he feeds me." Bianca said.

"And what about you, Daniel? How's it going on your end?" Michael asked.

"It's hard to complain after the first night here," Daniel said.

Michael, Mitch, and Alyssa hollered.

Bianca blushed.

"Wait, wasn't *I* in the tent that night?" Lauren asked.

"Were you? I didn't notice. I was focused on other things." Daniel said.

Bianca remained quiet.

"Oh, so that *was* you guys?" Mitch said.

"What, what do you mean?" Daniel said.

"Mitch swore it was Bianca and Lauren shaking the tent that night," Alyssa said.

"What the *fuck*?" Lauren said.

"Geez, Lauren, I'm not *that* gross," Bianca said.

"No, it's just-"

"I'm teasing," Bianca said.

"So what about last night?" Alyssa asked.

"Lauren was definitely in the tent last night," Daniel said.

"No action, then?" Mitch asked.

"Not that it's your business, but no. No action." Bianca said.

"I don't blame you. It's not like we have showers out here." Alyssa said. "I can't imagine any *action* being enjoyable."

"I wouldn't mind," Mitch said.

"It's for reasons like that, that you don't get any," Alyssa said. The group laughed.

Daniel squeezed Bianca. "Sounds like a lot of action will go on after we bathe in this lake, then."

"You wish you could be so lucky," Bianca said.

"You guys are so gross!" Lauren said.

"You sound like you could use a smoke." Mitch pulled a joint from his pocket.

"Really?" Lauren said.

"Mitch, stop. You're gonna corrupt that girl." Alyssa said.

"I think I already did," Mitch said.

Lauren grabbed the joint from his hand, and he lit it for her. "What can I say? I think I like it."

***

Camera 1

"Hey, you guys! Come look at this!" Michael yelled from behind the camera. He focused the footage on a footprint in the dirt. It seemed like it could've been that of a human, but it was fading away. The most prominent portion was where the big toe would be, but there was no sign of a heel. Footsteps could be heard as the rest of the group approached. "What do you guys think this footprint comes from?"

"Oh wow, let me see!" Winston pushed Michael away from the print.

Michael continued to film him as he examined it.

"This could be our first evidence of Bigfoot! I don't see any other prints nearby, but this one is certainly interesting." Winston said.

"Really? You see one footprint and assume it's Bigfoot's? For all we know, it's Bianca's from yesterday." Daniel said.

"No, no. Her toes are much smaller." Winston said.

"What are you, the foot inspector?" Bianca said.

"Do you care to try it? Step on the print. Prove my point." Winston said.

Bianca looked like she didn't want to do it, but she did. She lowered her injured foot onto the print, lining up her big toe with that of the print. She was careful not to put too much pressure on the injury. As Winston expected, her foot was much, much smaller.

"See, point proven," Winston said.

"Not really, it could be anybody's. Just because she has small toes doesn't mean a mythical creature is running around out here." Daniel said.

"Would someone with bigger shoes like to try?" Winston said.

"I will," Mitch said, stepping forward.

"No, thanks. The less your feet are in the documentary, the better." Daniel said.

"Winston does have a point, though. Sure, I'm not a good example, but that footprint is huge." Bianca said.

"How do we even know if it's a footprint? It's super faded! It could be anything." Daniel said.

"Open your mind, man," Mitch said.

"You guys are going to drive me crazy. Can we just get to the lake? Please?" Daniel said.

"Okay, but if you see any more footprints, let us know," Winston said.

***

Camera 1

The camera came on and had a great view of the lake from the dock.

"Who is gonna get in first?" Michael yelled, holding the camera. He aimed it at the rest of the group waiting around the beach.

Bianca was dipping her injured foot in the water, testing not only the temperature but also whether or not it would hurt if she submerged it.

Mitch was removing his shirt while Alyssa was laying down their towels.

"Feel free to do the honors!" Daniel said, laying down a towel of his own.

"Alright, so be it," Michael said, quiet enough that only the camera could hear it. He set the camera down on the dock, facing the length of the pier toward the beach. He pulled off his shirt and kicked off his shoes. He removed his socks and stuffed them in his right shoe, so he was down to nothing but the swimming trunks he had worn for the entire hike. He picked up the camera and brought it down the dock, placing it on the edge facing outward toward the lake. "Time to set an example." He said. He began yelling out a nonsense scream, and his footsteps could be heard as he ran behind the camera. He entered the frame from the top as he did a cannonball dive, jumping over the camera.

The water splashed the lens as he entered the lake, and the group on the beach all cheered for him.

His head erupted from the water, and he inhaled loudly. He wiped his hair backward and rubbed the water from his eyes. "Is someone gonna join me?" He yelled in the direction of the beach.

***

Camera 4

"*Someone* has to set our towels up!" Nancy yelled to Daniel.

This camera was placed on the floor beside Mitch's towel and had a clear view of the group and the lake.

"Suit yourself!" Michael's voice was quiet in the distance.

Daniel removed his shirt, and Mitch followed suit, only Daniel was already wearing swim trunks, and Mitch was in blue jeans.

"Are me and Michael the only two that brought bathing suits?" Daniel asked.

"Oh, no. I've got mine on under my clothes." Nancy said.

"Yeah, so do I," Mitch said, and without missing a beat, ripped his pants off, exposing his white briefs beneath them.

"Come on, seriously?" Winston said. "There are girls here. Have some decency."

"But I only see *you* complaining," Mitch said.

"Yeah, I'm with Mitch," Bianca said, pulling her pants down, wearing silk panties beneath.

"Woah," Nancy said, putting her hands up to block her close view of Bianca's backside.

"Mitch is right. I am not complaining." Daniel said as Bianca pulled her shirt up and over her head.

She kicked off her single shoe, removed her sock, and now down to only her bra and panties.

"What is happening right now?" Nancy asked.

Daniel offered his hand and led Bianca down the beach to the dock.

"Lauren, please tell me that you're gonna have a swimsuit when you unbutton that blouse?" Nancy said.

"What?" Lauren asked, her eyes struggling to stay open.

Mitch giggled. "I told you I corrupted her already." He pat Alyssa's shoulder and ran to the dock.

Meanwhile, Daniel pretended to push Bianca into the water, but he slipped on the wet surface caused by Michael splashing them both from below. Daniel fell back-first into the water. When he came up, he waved to Bianca to join him.

Bianca turned away from him, walking to the other side of the dock to unhook her bra. She dropped it to the floor and left her panties with it. Running as fast as she could with her injured foot, she leaped into the water, landing dangerously close to Daniel, nearly on his head.

"Who even *is* that girl? That is not the Bianca I grew up with!" Nancy said.

"Hell yeah!" Mitch yelled, kicking off his briefs before getting to the dock. Completely naked, he ran straight into the water.

Winston's face turned sour.

"Your turn, Alyssa!" Mitch yelled.

"You're not going to, are you?" Nancy asked.

"I mean, why not? It'll be fun." Alyssa smiled.

"If it was just Michael and me, then *maybe*. But you really want everyone here to see you naked?"

"I don't see what the big deal is. Don't you just feel *free* with your clothes off? And what better place than somewhere out in the open world? And we're all friends here. It's not like we're with a bunch of strangers."

"Sure, we're friends, but I never thought I'd want to get to know you guys *that* much."

"Just don't think about it like that."

"It's kind of hard not to."

They could hear cheering from the lake.

Without making a sound, Lauren had found her way onto the dock, unbuttoning her blouse and kicking off her shoes.

"Look at that! Even she's joining us!" Mitch said.

Daniel and Michael followed, pulled their bottoms out from beneath the water, and threw them.

By the time their trunks made it onto the dock, Lauren was nude and diving into the water.

"I can't believe this," Winston said.

"You're not going to join us?" Alyssa asked.

"No thanks. I'll keep my clothes *on*, thank you very much." Winston said.

"Okay, suit yourself." Alyssa stood up and unbuttoned her pants.

Mitch whistled from the lake.

"Tell me you'll come," Alyssa said.

"I think I'll just dip my feet. That water looks cold," Nancy said.

"Lame," Alyssa said, removing the last of her clothes.

Nancy looked away from her.

Winston stared at her closely between hard stares at the girls in the water.

"Hey, bring the radio!" Mitch pointed to the radio that sat behind their towel.

Alyssa grabbed it and ran out toward the dock.

Nancy stripped down to her lime green two-piece bathing seat and followed her.

***

Camera 1

The camera had a great view of the group enjoying themselves on the water. Alyssa sat atop Mitch's shoulders and Bianca on Daniel's while they had a "chicken fight." The radio was somewhere behind the camera playing "Every Breath You Take" by The Police. Everybody was laughing.

Lauren was wide-awake as her high had worn off, and she joined Michael in splashing the two couples.

Bianca was the first to fall, and she brought Daniel beneath the water with her when she did.

Nancy sat on the edge of the dock beside the camera, the only one by the water with their suit still on. She kicked her legs up and down in the water, making light splashes. She screamed when Michael's head appeared between her feet and emerged from the water.

"Don't do that!" She yelled.

"Why don't you join us?" He asked.

"I'm fine up here, thanks."

"But we're all having so much fun."

"Yeah, but there's less risk of running into penis up here."

"Weird, I didn't think you were scared of them. Actually, I always thought you were particularly fond of them."

"Screw you." She laughed.

"Come on, what's it going to take?" He asked. "At least get in the water."

"Then I'll be the odd one out."

"There's only one way to fix that." He pushed off the small bit of dock between her legs and floated back toward the rest of the group. "Take it off! Take it off! Take it off!" He pumped his fist in the air with each word as he chanted.

The rest of them in the water joined in the chant. "Take it off! Take it off! Take it off!"

Nancy pulled at the string on the back of her bikini top, unraveling it and letting it hang down the front of her chest.

The chant continued with mixed yelling and whistling.

Nancy stood up, shaking her head. She pulled her bottoms off, kicked them to the side, finished pulling her top over her head, and threw it out of the camera's view somewhere along the dock.

The chanting turned into clapping and cheering as she dove into the water.

Interviewer: *It would seem like peer pressure is big for this group.*

Nancy: *That's just how it was. Nobody ever meant any harm. It may not be my proudest moment, but it was a lot of fun.*

Interviewer: *Do you regret it?*

Nancy: *Not at all. Sure, I was too caught in the moment to think about the cameras, but this was just a group of friends having fun. One of the few good memories from this trip. I just wish it could've stayed that way.*

Interviewer: *What way?*

Nancy: *A memory.*

***

Camera 4

Winston brought his camera out onto the dock.

"Get that camera out of here, you perv!" Bianca splashed water toward him.

"Yeah, you can't just film us and not *join* us!" Alyssa said.

"You're all on camera, *anyways*. This one's pointed right at you!" Winston pointed to Michael's camera on the dock. "Besides, I'm trying to film a documentary, remember?"

"Oh yeah, what's it about? Human anatomy?" Bianca asked.

"You guys quit teasing him. Come on, Winston! Get in here with us!" Lauren said.

"No thanks. Not my kind of party." Winston said.

The group groaned.

"Really? You've got a single, hot, *naked* woman telling you she wants you to strip and have some fun with her, and you won't oblige?" Michael said.

"Please, stop asking me to take my clothes off. It's getting weird." Winston said.

"At this point, it's weird that you're the only one with your clothes *on*," Michael said.

"Whatever." Winston brought the camera back down the dock while they all yelled taunts at him. He returned to where all their towels were and grabbed a water bottle from his backpack. "Okay, viewers. Even though this documentary was Michael's idea, I will be the only one to try and get something worth watching for you."

***

Camera 4

Winston brought the camera with him into the woods. He followed what looked like a path, but it was away from the stream that brought them to the lake, to begin with. "I'm watching the floor closely, hoping to find more prints similar to the one we saw earlier. Maybe one that's more clear." He held the camera in front of himself, focusing on the floor below. "I don't think the lake is a bad place to look for a creature like this. If he's anything like a human, he would need water. The forest nearby would be a great spot for him to live if my idiot friends didn't scare him away with all of that noise."

The wind howled above him. The dirt scraped beneath his combat boots.

"It might be best if I get off of this trail. It's too open. If Bigfoot sees me first, he might get spooked and run away."

Winston brought the camera off trail, squeezing between two bushes and crunching all the leaves and twigs he could in the process. He set the camera on the floor beside himself and stretched his arms out wide. His trench coat flapped in the wind like a flag on a pole. His stomach hung out beneath his t-shirt.

"Let me tell you, this hiking stuff is hard work." Winston sat down next to the bush he had crawled past before. He stared through it. "Maybe I'll hide here and observe nature. See if anything alarming pops up."

He sat there for upwards of twenty minutes, only moving occasionally to take a sip from his bottle, and only spoke every couple of minutes to spew some nonsense fact about Bigfoot that sounded like he made it up. Rather than getting bored and leaving his spot, he fell asleep.

The familiar but loud sounds of leaves crunching below footsteps woke him up. He sat up without urgency and did his usual morning yawn before he heard it again. That was when he looked around, acknowledging the bush in front of him, and remembered where he was.

"Hello?" He asked.

There was no response.

Twigs cracked, and leaves flew around with a gust of wind.

"Is someone out here? You guys better not be fucking with me." He said. "Stupid pranks."

The next sound of footprints came from right behind the camera. Winston was looking in the opposite direction.

A loud snarl followed by an exhale came next.

This time, Winston heard it. He was slow to turn around. Once he died, his eyes spread open. "Oh, shit!" He looked down at the camera and tried to run to it, but he tripped and fell to the floor.

Whatever it was that had Winston spooked grabbed him by his arm that lay outside of the camera's view.

Winston screamed as it pulled him past the camera.

Nancy: *Oh my God.*

Interviewer: *You haven't seen this yet, have you?*

Nancy: *No. I've done my best not to watch **any** of this.*

Interviewer: *The rest of this might be hard for you. We can turn it off.*

Nancy: *No, I'll be okay. I have to see exactly what happened to them.*

Indistinguishable sounds followed. The loudest of them all was Winston's screams that went on for a minute, only to be silenced by one loud crack. A bloodstream trailed into the camera's point of view as it poured in across the leaves.

The camera saw nothing but picked up disturbing audio of Winston's flesh being ripped apart by the beast. It was breathing like a rabid dog while it chewed apart its prey.

Then, Winston's detached arm flew into view, landing just in front of the camera, the trench coat sleeve still attached. Speckles of blood splashed the camera lens when it plopped onto the floor.

Interviewer: *Are you okay?*

Nancy: *That ... was rough*

Interviewer: *Can we get you anything?*

Nancy: *No thanks, I'll be fine. If he can go through ... that, I can go through this.*

Interviewer: *Are you sure?*

Nancy: *Yes. Plus, I'm sure it only gets worse from here.*

Interviewer: *You might be right on that. Let us know if you need to stop, take a break, or do anything else.*

Nancy: *Does this camera show anything else?*

Interviewer: *Not for a while.*

Nancy: *Okay, roll the next one.*

***

Camera 3

The camera hadn't moved, but the group had. Mitch was lying on his towel now, with another across his pubic region.

Alyssa lay beside him, equally naked but without a towel for cover.

The rest of them were drying off and getting their clothes back on.

"This is what life's about," Mitch said.

"Isn't it just nice to be so free?" Alyssa said.

Mitch pulled out a joint and started to light it.

"Where did you even grab that from?" Alyssa asked.

"My pocket."

Alyssa lifted his towel to see if he had put something containing pockets on when she wasn't looking, but he hadn't.

"Hey, watch it!" Mitch said, pulling the towel back down.

"Sorry, I- you know what? Never mind." Alyssa said.

Nancy: *Where **did** he grab that from?*

Interviewer: *Not a clue.*

"Did you see Lauren out there?" Mitch asked.

"What about her?" Alyssa asked.

"She's a lot of fun when you get her out of her thick shell," Mitch said. "Maybe she's not so much of a good girl after all."

"You're going to ruin that girl's life if you keep it up."

"I'd say I'm making it better. She had the time of her life out there. Honestly, I'd be surprised if she'd *ever* gotten that naked before, even alone."

"I'm sure she does."

"Well, either way. If that's what ruining a life looks like, sign me up. We need to ruin Winston's next."

"I'm not so sure we can. I've never met someone with as thick of a skull as him." Alyssa said.

"Hey, now that you mention it," Nancy said, drying her hair a few feet away from them, "Where is Winston?"

Alyssa sat up and looked around. "That's weird. His stuff is still over there." She pointed to the backpack that he had left behind.

"Yeah, but his camera's not." Michael walked up from the beach. He looked at Mitch. "You gonna put your clothes back on?"

"We're working on our tans," Alyssa said as if she wasn't tan already.

"You, I don't have a problem with. In fact, I'd prefer it if you stayed that way for the rest of the trip-"

"Michael!" Nancy smacked his chest with the back of her hand.

Alyssa pulled her towel up to cover up.

"-but Mitch, please put some pants on." Michael finished.

"Why? Are we leaving already?" Mitch asked.

"Not necessarily, but we might have to look for Winston," Michael said.

"Hey, Lauren!" Nancy yelled to her on the beach.

Lauren looked over at her.

"Do you know where Winston went?" Nancy asked.

"No, why would I?" Lauren asked.

Nancy shrugged.

"All of the naked girls probably scared him away!" Bianca yelled from the beach. Her pale skin grew alarmingly red in the sun.

"He probably went back to camp!" Daniel yelled.

"He's right," Michael said.

"Still, it wouldn't be right if we didn't at least spend *some* time looking for him," Nancy said. "Come on, Alyssa, put some clothes on, and let's see if we can find him."

Alyssa's shoulders fell in disappointment. "My guess is he's probably looking for more Bigfoot evidence."

"Okay, but he won't be able to find his way back if we leave him here," Nancy said.

"Fine, but only if you promise we come back by the end of the trip."

"We have a few days left," Nancy started to whisper, "I'm sure the boys won't have any problems with doing this again."

"I know I wouldn't," Mitch said.

"I hope not." Alyssa got up. She was already dry from the sun, so she went straight into slipping back into her clothes.

While Mitch got dressed, Daniel, Bianca, and Lauren approached from the beach.

"So, I have an idea," Daniel said. "Winston's probably going to come back soon. I don't think he would make it long in the woods alone. While we wait for him to come back, how about I cook us some lunch? I don't want to do it close to our camp anymore, and this seems perfect. We're all tired, anyways. I know I'm not in the mood to walk back to lug all this back to camp right now."

"That sounds great," Michael said.

"I could use a minute to sit down," Bianca said. "My foot is killing me."

"So we're not gonna look for Winston?" Nancy asked.

"He's a big boy. For all we know, he's just using the bathroom." Daniel said.

"With a camera?" Nancy asked.

"We can watch our recorded footage on them, right? He's probably watching us skinny-dip right now. You know, touching himself." Bianca said, finishing her sentence by flicking her tongue from beneath her upper lip.

"Ew!" Lauren said.

"I hope not," Nancy said. "See, that's why I didn't want to do this!"

"You don't think he really is, right?" Lauren asked.

"Who knows? I'm just saying he could be." Bianca said.

Nancy: *At this point, I* **wish** *that was what he was doing.*

"No matter *what* he's doing, I'm sure he will be back soon. Until then, let's try not to worry about it." Daniel said.

Over the next hour, they waited for Winston while Daniel cooked hot dogs for them on his stovetop. Winston never came back.

Chapter 12

Night Terrors

Camera 1

"Can we worry about Winston now?" Nancy asked, pointing the camera at Michael's face.

"I wouldn't. I'm sure he just went back to camp. It's about time we do the same before it gets too dark." Michael said.

"Yep, pack it up, everyone!" Daniel said.

"Wait, really?" Bianca asked. She looked feverish. Sweat covered her forehead, her visible skin burnt from the sun, her hair unkempt, and she lacked any energy, but she didn't have any vocal complaints.

"Yeah, it will be way too dark in about an hour. Now is best. Don't worry, I'll help you walk, and if you need to stop for a breather, we can." Daniel said.

"I'll be okay."

They packed their towels into their bags, packed what hot dogs and drinks remained into the ice chest, and headed back to the camp. They stopped multiple times along the way to check on Bianca, but she insisted that she was okay every time.

Nancy: *By now, I think we memorized the way back to camp. Well, most of us did. Luckily, because that hike would've taken forever, and I'm not so sure Bianca was up to it. She said she was fine, but she was struggling. I think her foot must've developed an infection or something.*

The sun was beginning to set when they arrived back at the camp. The sun looked bright red in the sky, an indicator that the next day would be hot. But that wasn't what was most alarming to them.

Instead, it was the fact that somebody had raided their camp. Their tents ransacked, their clothes thrown all around, and their air mattresses slashed and flattened along with three tires on Michael's truck. They smashed Mitch's headlights and threw a brick through the windshield.

"Who the fuck did this?" Michael yelled. He rummaged through the damage, throwing his hands in the air every few moments, completely freaking out. He was searching for answers, and there weren't any.

"Where is Winston?" Lauren asked.

"You don't think he did this, did you?" Bianca asked

"I'll fucking kill him," Michael said.

Nancy brought the camera into her tent. Winston's stuff was still there and tossed around like the rest of theirs. "It wasn't him! His stuff is all here, trashed like the rest."

"He could've done that on purpose, to throw us off his trail," Daniel said.

"How would he expect to get home? He doesn't have a car!" Nancy said. "I know he may not be the smartest of the bunch, but he's not stupid."

"So, who was it then?" Michael got in Nancy's face.

"How the fuck am I supposed to know?"

"Michael, calm down. You aren't the only one who's mad right now." Bianca said.

Michael walked away from Nancy, shaking his head. "If I find out who did this... I swear to God."

Nancy picked the camera back up.

"It was probably some asshole teenagers," Alyssa said.

"So, what are we going to do? Are we supposed to sleep here tonight?" Lauren asked.

"It's gonna be hard to leave without my tires," Michael said.

An engine revving caught the attention of Nancy, who pointed the camera to Mitch's van, where he sat in the driver's seat. He honked the horn.

"My van still works!" Mitch said.

"At least we can make a few trips to get us all out of here," Daniel said.

"I hate to say it, but I think finding Winston is more important," Bianca said.

"And how are we supposed to do that? It's going to be pitch-black out here in half an hour."

"What, do we just leave him in the woods to fend for himself?" Lauren asked. "Why don't we go to the park ranger and see if they can help us find him?"

"Look at Mitch's van. The headlights are out. They won't be able to get back here once it gets dark. It's too dangerous.

If Winston gets back to the lake and sees that we aren't there, he will make his way back to camp. We will wake up early tomorrow, and if he isn't back, we will look for him." Daniel said.

The rest stayed silent.

"It's the best we can do. Unless anybody has any other suggestions?" Daniel said.

They did not.

"Alright, everybody, start packing your bags. Check to make sure that whoever did this didn't steal anything. One way or another, this trip is over tomorrow." Daniel said.

Interviewer: *Don't take offense to this, but were you all really okay with this plan? I mean, leaving him in the woods overnight?*

Nancy: *Okay with it? No, of course not. I wasn't okay with **any** of this. We didn't see any better options, unfortunately.*

***

Camera 2

"Nope. Nothing's missing." Bianca said. The camera sat in the corner of their tent, and she had just finished packing her clothing back into her bag. She sat where the now flattened air mattress used to be while Daniel rolled it up.

"My stuff's all here, too," Lauren said

"That's just so weird. Why would they destroy our stuff and not take any?" Daniel said.

"Hey, what's this?" When Daniel picked up the air mattress, Bianca picked up a piece of paper that fell onto the ground.

"Is it a note?" Daniel asked.

Lauren crawled over to look at it while Bianca read it.

"It says, 'I tried to warn you before, and it didn't work. I'm sorry, but you left me with no other choice.'" Bianca's eyes narrowed in confusion. "Any idea who could've written this?"

"Not a fucking clue. Are they serious?" Daniel said. "They come into our camp, destroy our shit, and have the audacity to leave us a note-"

"-I know who did it." Lauren interrupted.

***

Camera 1

"Look, see." Nancy's hand extended into the camera's view, where she pointed at Winston's belongings on their tent floor. "His stuff is all here. He couldn't have done this."

"Then who did?" Michael yelled.

"I don't know! None of us do, and we might never know. But you don't have to be mean to me. We are *all* upset, okay? Don't take that shit out on me." Nancy said.

He looked at her on the verge of tears. "You're right."

"What?

"I shouldn't take it out on you. You're right, and I'm sorry." He reached his arms out, and she tried to help pull him up, but instead, he pulled her in for a hug. "I'm just frustrated."

"I know me too. Trust me. But we need to be there for each other, not take it out on each other. Okay?"

"Okay.

Nancy: *I was absolutely stunned when he pulled me in like that. I had never seen him handle his anger so well. Honestly, I forgot about this moment until now.*

"Michael!" Daniel yelled from outside their tent.

"What?" Michael said.

Nancy turned the camera to the tent entrance, where Daniel swung open the flaps. Bianca and Lauren stood behind him.

"We know who did this to our campsite," Daniel said.

"What? Who?" Michael asked.

Daniel handed him the note that they found in their tent. "We found this."

Michael read it, mumbling the words too quietly for anyone else to hear. "What? What does this mean? This doesn't tell me anything."

"Remember that creepy old guy we saw at the gas station the other day? Doesn't this sound like him?" Lauren said.

Anger filled Michael's eyes. "I'll kill him."

"What's going on? What did the note even say?" Nancy asked.

"Something about warning us? I don't know, here." Michael handed it to her. "It's fucking nonsense. This *has* to have been him."

Nancy read the note.

"So what do we do?" Bianca asked.

"Do we go to the police?" Lauren asked.

"I doubt they will help. That guy probably lives in the middle of the forest, living off the land or something. He's probably the one that set our camp on fire." Michael said.

"Do you think he killed Tommy and Cindy?" Bianca asked.

"I wouldn't put it past him. The guy's a total creep." Michael reached for his backpack and pulled out several large hunting knives. "Here, each of you take one. Keep yourselves safe tonight. Hand one to Mitch on the way back to your tent, too."

"Is that necessary?" Nancy asked.

"Some crackhead is running around out here threatening us. I'd say it's necessary." Daniel said.

"Try not to poke yourself with it," Michael said when Lauren grabbed hers.

"Alright, you guys get some sleep tonight. We wake up early tomorrow, find Winston, and get the *fuck* out of here." Daniel said.

***

Camera 2

"Fuck this trip," Daniel said. The camera filmed them lying on the floor of their tent with the night vision filter while they tried to sleep.

"You're finally thinking that?" Bianca asked.

"I've been thinking it since he slashed my mattress. I would've rather he stole from me. Messing with my sleep comfort is an entirely different level of disrespect." Daniel said. "I'm gonna be limping around like you tomorrow after this floor messes up my back."

"Do we have to listen to you complain all night?" Bianca asked.

"Only until I fall asleep. I can think of a few ways you could make that happen quicker." He smiled, but she likely didn't see it.

"Gross," Lauren said.

"On the floor? That's only a guarantee to mess up your back."

"I tried." Daniel rolled over, facing opposite Bianca. "If I die tonight, don't resuscitate me unless you can guarantee I'll have a bed to sleep in."

"I don't see what the big deal is. I've been sleeping on the floor for this whole trip!"

"It's not a big deal. Daniel's just a big baby." Bianca crawled to the opposite end of her blanket, leaning toward where Lauren had been lying the whole time. "So, what's up with this bad girl phase you're going through?"

"What do you mean?" Lauren asked.

"You know what I mean. It started with the smoking. Then you were out there skinny dipping with the rest of us ... I don't know, the whole thing just feels out of character for you."

"I'm just having fun. I've never done half of the stuff that I've gotten to on this trip, and I'm enjoying it."

"Is that right? Just trying new things?"

"Yeah, why not? We are in the middle of nowhere, away from the rest of the world. What better time than now?"

"That's a good point. How about we try something new tonight?"

"What did you have in mind?"

Bianca leaned in close to her and whispered loud enough for Daniel to hear, "Have you ever slept with a girl?"

Daniel sat up to a perfect ninety-degree angle.

Lauren looked as shocked as a deer in headlights.

Nancy: *I don't know what I thought Bianca was going to say, but it sure wasn't that. And by the look on Lauren's face, I can't tell if she's more shocked or intrigued.*

"I ... I wasn't ... I'm not-" Lauren stuttered.

Bianca fell onto her back, laughing and kicking her working foot. "I'm just fucking with you! But you were totally up for it! I like this new Lauren."

"No, I-"

"You don't have to say anything. As I said, I was messing with you." Bianca sat back up.

Daniel laid back down.

Lauren's face turned depressed.

"Oh my gosh, what's wrong? I didn't mean to hurt your feelings! It was only a joke." Bianca said.

"No, it's not that. You're totally fine."

"Then what's wrong?"

"It's just ... we're in here, joking and smiling and having fun, but I almost feel guilty about it. What if Winston isn't okay? Even if he's unhurt, he could be lost out there in the wilderness while we are in here safe. I was having the *best* time of my entire life out on the lake, and we didn't even notice that he had left! I can't help but-"

"-Hey, hey, hey, stop that. Don't do that." Bianca interrupted. "Don't beat yourself up over something that you are unsure of. Bad things happen all the time, trust me. I've had my fair share of love and loss, but at the end of the day, we have to live while we are here. Mourn when bad things happen, but enjoy life when it's appropriate. Even if the things we're doing are inappropriate."

"I know, it's just-"

"-Nope. I know this whole bad girl thing is new to you, but the best part about that personality is to learn when not to care. I'm sure Winston is okay. Twenty-four hours from now, we will all be back at Nancy's house, laughing about the stuff that went on during the trip. Right now, enjoy it while we can."

"Okay. You're right."

"I know I am!"

"Thank you. Seriously."

"No problem. I'll stop flirting with you for the night so you can get some sleep, and we will find him in the morning."

"Did you say flirting? When were you-"

"Good night." Bianca laid down.

"Good night." Lauren zipped up her sleeping bag, and they went to sleep.

***

Camera 3

The camera sat in its usual spot that Mitch would have in their tent at night. Alyssa and Mitch were lying together on the floor beneath the blankets that the fire had ruined.

"My feet are *so* sore," Mitch said. "Seriously, I think they're as bad as Bianca's."

"That's what happens when you don't wear shoes on a hike." Alyssa rolled away from him. Her eyes were closed.

Mitch rolled over with her, wrapping his arm around her body as they entered a spooning position. "Do you think Winston's okay?"

"I hope so." Alyssa kicked her legs, struggling to get the blanket to cover her feet. "We need to get some sleep so we can have enough energy to find him in the morning."

"Have you been having a good time on this trip?"

Alyssa's eyebrow twitched. "Today was nice. I'm glad everyone was comfortable enough to have fun at the lake and not make it weird. I'm not enjoying myself so much since we got back, though."

"I'm sorry."

"Don't be. It's not your fault."

"Tomorrow, everything will work itself out. I promise. And a month from now, we will go on an even bigger vacation, just the two of us."

"That sounds nice."

"Yeah, it does. I love you."

"I love you too. Get some sleep."

Mitch was already sleeping before he could hear her.

***

Camera 1

The camera faced Nancy while she tried to sleep.

Michael tossed and turned behind her.

"I guess it's not *all* bad." Michael broke the long silence.

"What?" Nancy said.

"With Winston out of the tent," he wrapped his arm around her stomach and pulled her closer to him, "we finally have some alone time."

She pushed his arm off of her. "Yeah, that means one less person is snoring to keep me awake."

"Seriously?"

"Yes."

"But we-"

"I'm just not in the mood, okay? I had all of my personal belongings run through by some crazy old man, and one of our friends is missing, but above all else, I am fucking *exhausted*. Sex is the absolute *last* thing on my mind right now."

"When you say that, I sound like an asshole."

"Maybe you are. Can I please get some sleep?"

"Suit yourself." Michael threw the blanket off of himself and got up. He picked up the camera and started unzipping the tent.

"Where are you going?" Nancy asked.

He pointed the camera at her.

"I've got to piss."

"With the camera?"

"The night vision will help me. Besides, it's not doing any good *in* the tent. I'm gonna place it outside so it can catch any campsite intruders. You know, just in case."

"Good idea."

The camera flickered into night vision mode, and he brought it about five trees deep into the woods and sat it down at his feet. The camera could hear him shuffling his pajama bottoms, and not soon after, a stream of liquid was flowing from the top left of the screen to the floor. Michael was letting out moans of relief while he emptied his bladder.

"Is someone there?" Michael asked.

The camera could not hear or see anything at all.

"Nancy, did you follow me out here?" He said. "What the-"

A muffled thud silenced his voice. His upper torso fell into the camera's view, landing face-first in his mess of urine. He was still breathing as his back heaved on the floor, but he was unconscious. His assailant dragged him out of view, his arms being the last piece of him in sight before he was gone.

Interviewer: *Are you okay?*

Nancy: ...

Interviewer: *Do you need to take a break?*

Nancy: *No. Let's just move on.*

Interviewer: *Are you sure?*

Nancy: *Please. Let's get this over with.*

Interviewer: *We are getting pretty close to the end. Would you like to tell me how you're feeling right now?*

Nancy: *No. No, I wouldn't. Play the next tape. Just play them all.*

Chapter 13

The Search

Camera 2

The night turned to day as the sun shone through Daniel's thin tent fabric, but that wasn't enough to wake them up. It wasn't until Nancy was screaming in the distance that Daniel jumped out of bed and picked up the camera to see what was wrong.

He ran into the woods, where he found Nancy hysterically crying and clawing at her hair above Michael's camera on the dirt floor. "Nancy? What's wrong?"

Nancy stuttered through uncontrollable breaths and tears.

"Breathe, okay? What happened? Where's Michael?" Daniel asked.

Mitch and Alyssa walked into the frame.

Alyssa's hair was a knotted mess, and she was rubbing her eyes.

Mitch didn't look to be any more tired than usual.

"I don't know," Nancy said. Her hyperventilating relaxed. "He came out here to pee last night and never came back! I just found his camera here." She picked up the camera and showed it to them.

"Really?" Daniel asked.

"Woah," Mitch said.

"Fuck! This trip just keeps getting worse." Daniel said.

"We have to go out there and find him!" Nancy stood to her feet and turned away, as if she was going to wander into the woods without a plan.

"Wait, slow down. What about Winston? Did he come back last night?" Daniel said.

Nancy stopped and looked horrified. "No. Oh my God, I didn't even think about him! He's got to be in danger!"

"Stop freaking out! Let me think." Everyone went quiet and waited for Daniel to continue. "Okay, I got it."

"A plan?" Alyssa asked.

"Yes. Mitch and I will head into the woods. Alyssa will take their van and try to find the ranger station. Tell them we need a whole search party. Nancy, you are staying here with Lauren and Bianca. Watch the camp, make sure the old guy doesn't fuck with us anymore, and make sure Bianca is okay. She is good at hiding it, but I think her foot is really bothering her." Daniel took a breath. "Any questions?"

"I'm going with you," Nancy said.

"No, you're not. No offense, but I don't think you would be much help if you're freaking out like this. You will be better off here, especially if Michael returns before we do." Daniel said.

"Yeah, he's right. He and Mitch will be fine, Nancy. They will find him faster than anyone else." Alyssa said.

"Okay. Just ... bring them back." Nancy said.

***

Camera 4

The camera had remained still all night, but someone picked it up as soon as morning hit.

"What's this?" As the camera waved, a man's voice mumbled, catching blurry glimpses of tattered boots against the dirt.

Once the camera settled, the holder carried it through the woods. The man walked with a hustle, failing to get a clear view of anything through the camera's lens for at least twenty minutes.

Once the footage settled, it focused on Nancy and Lauren sitting around the empty fire pit. Lauren had her arm around Nancy, who rocked back and forth in her seat, too anxious to sit still.

"Why are they still here?" The man's voice spoke before he turned the camera to face himself. It was the older man that they had their altercation with at the gas station. "I warned them. I fucking warned them." He pointed the camera forward again and walked around the camp's perimeter. "Now they're dead. They're *all* dead-" The camera jolted toward tree branches cracking. The man crept toward a bush in that direction and pointed the camera through.

Less than fifteen yards in that direction, Bianca was squatting beside a tree, her pants pulled below her knees. She looked nervous and in pain. The camera stayed on her for five seconds before the sound of her urination began. Bianca must have heard something because she started to lean her head, peeking toward the camera.

The man pulled the camera away, keeping it low to the ground as he left. The footage was shaky for another six minutes before it settled on a fading trail of blood that the man found. It was unclear where the path started or headed, as the wind had blown the leaves around the area since the stains were left, but he followed it as close as he could. It led him to a tree that had fallen over. The trail made it clear that the assailant had dragged the victim over the trunk.

"Shit!" The man yelled and fell to the floor when he came close to the tree. "What did I say?" He brought the camera over the trunk, and a corpse was on the other side.

The face had been crushed and devoured, its limbs had been mangled, and its insides outward. If it weren't for his pajama bottoms, there would be no other features remaining to help identify that it was Michael.

"I warned you, but you didn't listen." The man took the camera away from Michael's body and walked through the forest. "You kids think you're the first ones to come out here? Of course not! And I'm sure you won't be the last. That last group disturbed her peace, and now she's angry. I tried to warn you, but I will *not* sit around and let her get me, *too*. Oh, no. I'm going to grab my shit and leave. I just wish you did the same."

He turned the camera to the sound of a man shrieking in pain. "Fuck!" He changed his walk to a sprint. After a few minutes of shaky footage, he placed the camera on the floor of a lime-green tent that did not belong to any campers. The man began piling clothes from the floor into a plastic grocery bag.

There was another scream.

"I don't have time." He ran out of the tent. Clothes fell out of his bag, but he did not stop to grab them.

***

Camera 2

Daniel left Mitch in charge of the camera so he could be as attentive to the search as possible.

"What are you thinking?" Mitch asked.

Daniel was squatting over the area where Nancy found Michael's camera. "I'm not thinking much. There's no sign of anything. We might have to head into the woods and call their names. Maybe go towards the lake in case Winston stayed there overnight."

"I should put some shoes on, then," Mitch said.

"Yeah, you should," Daniel said.

Mitch handed him the camera.

Daniel began filming the ground while he waved away the leaves on the floor. He prepared to stand up before his last swipe exposed something that caught his attention. "No way." He focused the camera and cleared the spot entirely of leaves.

There was a large footprint. It looked similar in size to the one they had found the day before, but this one was clearer in shape. It was at least twenty inches in length from toe to heel and six inches in width. It looked almost human but more feral. The ends of the toes had a shape that looked like it was from a hard claw of some sort. The edges of the entire print were less round and more jagged.

"It can't be," Daniel said. He pointed the camera around the surrounding area, using his shoe to kick the leaves out of the way, but this was the lone spot of mud that was soft enough to pick up a print. He turned the camera to Mitch, who was approaching and back to the print. He covered it with leaves again.

"Did you find something?" Mitch asked.

"Nope. Nothing." Daniel said.

"Okay, so are you ready to go?"

"Yeah, let's do it." Daniel pointed the camera toward the print one last time, then back to the camp.

Alyssa waved to them from the van's driver's seat and drove away.

"I'm gonna marry that girl," Mitch said.

Daniel turned away from the camp and started his walk through the woods. "Really? Are you sure you're ready for that kind of commitment?"

"Am I ready for it? Hell, I'm already committed. I have been since we met."

"Yeah, but marriage is a whole different ball game. It's more final."

"That's what I want! She's made me this happy up until now. I'd be an idiot not to lock that in."

"And what about her? Do you think that's something she wants?"

"She's stuck around this long. It's hard to believe she would deal with me for this long if she didn't."

"I know, but you guys are young. She has a whole life ahead of her to want to try new things. I mean, you saw how she was when she kissed Bianca. That didn't look like someone willing to sign their life away at the drop of a hat. She's a wild child."

"That kiss was just her way of teasing me. The best thing about our relationship is our comfort with each other. If she needed some time to try things out with women, she could be my guest, but that's not something she's looking for. We just like to have fun, and that is something that we always do together."

"Whatever you say, man. When do you plan on doing it?"

"Doing what?"

"Proposing!"

"Oh, right!" Mitch reached into the pocket of his shirt and pulled out a ring.

Daniel focused the camera on it. It was a slim band with a single diamond. It wasn't too impressive, but it shined beautifully against Mitch's dirty fingers.

"Woah, let me see that! Hold this." Daniel handed Mitch the camera, and he took the ring to examine it up close.

"I was going to do it on this trip, but everything fell apart. I never found a great time to do it."

"You should've done it at the lake, man! This ring is nice." Daniel slipped the ring back into Mitch's shirt.

"I thought about it, but none of us had clothes on. I figured since it was going to be captured on camera, I wanted the moment not to have so many penises in view. Maybe that way, our kids could watch it. By the time we had our clothes back on,

Winston was missing, and I wanted everyone to be there. Even if that guy is pretty weird."

"Fair enough. Once we find everyone, I'll set up a nice dinner for everyone back at camp, and you could do it then! Or maybe even at Michael's when we all get home. However you want to do it, I want to help."

"That sounds great, but I think I've got other plans. Alyssa and I will go on our own trip after this, and I'll do it then. There's just too much negativity here. I want our engagement not to be tied with any bad memories. But thank you."

"That sounds nice. I hope she says yes. You guys deserve it."

"Thank you."

"Wait." Daniel stopped in his tracks, holding his fist up. "Did you hear that?"

"Hear what-"

Daniel's eyes widened as he looked past the camera toward the sounds of an animal charging at them. Daniel could be seen sprinting away just before the camera tried to turn toward the sound.

Mitch shrieked, and the camera flew from his hand and landed in the dirt, cracking the lens. Solid green and blue colors filled the footage and took up most of the screen, occasionally flickering to show glimpses of the scene.

Daniel was running without looking back while the camera could hear the sounds of Mitch's bones cracking and flesh splitting apart.

It didn't go on for long. The glitches in the visuals only gave brief and indistinguishable glimpses of the animal that began to charge after Daniel. It had brown fur that resembled a grizzly bear's, only this creature was bipedal and larger than any bear.

The footage went black before it caught up to Daniel.

Nancy: *Jesus. I don't get it.*

Interviewer: *What don't you get?*

Nancy: *How can so many people watch this, and see ... well, that! But, they still deny that Bigfoot exists.*

Interviewer: *Technology has come a long way. Footage can be doctored to show anything, you know that.*

Nancy: *But this happened in 1983! Do they really think we could've edited this back then?*

Interviewer: *Who's to say? They did it in the movies.*

Nancy: *Bullshit. Just play the next tape.*

***

Camera 1

The girls at the camp heard Mitch's screaming. They didn't know it was his, but they heard it. Bianca held the camera in her lap while they sat around the fire pit.

"Okay, fuck this." Nancy stood up.

"What was that?" Lauren asked.

"I don't know, but I'm not gonna just wait here," Nancy said.

"What are you gonna do?" Bianca asked.

"I'm gonna go find our friends. Someone is in pain out there. They need us."

"Alyssa went to get help! I don't think it's smart to run out there by yourself." Lauren said.

"But we don't know when that help will arrive. What if they need immediate attention? Look, I'm not asking you to come with me. I'm just going to go real quick and see what's wrong." Nancy tied her hair back into a curly ponytail.

"But what if it was that crazy old man? He's probably still out there!" Lauren said.

"I'm not afraid of him." Nancy started to walk toward the woods.

"Wait-" Bianca got up to go after her but winced at the pain of putting her injured foot in the dirt. "Ouch!"

"Bianca, are you okay?" Nancy turned around and looked at her foot. She got to her knees and grabbed Bianca's ankle so that she could examine the injury. "Your foot is on *fire*. You need to rest. Trust me. I'll be okay. As soon as Alyssa gets back here, let whoever she brings to know that you need medical attention." Nancy stood back up. "Lauren, stay with her. Make sure she doesn't go anywhere."

"How about we all stay here?" Lauren asked.

"I think that sounds great," Bianca said.

"I know, but if that were Michael screaming out there, I would never be able to forgive myself. I have to go." Nancy walked reluctantly to the edge of their camp and looked back at them.

They heard the next scream.

"Was that Daniel?" Bianca asked.

"Stay here. I'll be back, I promise!" Nancy said and disappeared into the woods.

"She's going to get herself killed," Bianca said. "Ow, fuck!" She pointed the camera to her foot, where Lauren began unwrapping the bandage. Once it was off, she lifted her foot so the camera could see the injury on the bottom of it. It wasn't a big cut, no bigger than a quarter in size. The center was a dark red chunk of dried blood, covered loosely by yellow, infected skin trying to grow back. The surrounding area was inflamed, leaving the entirety of the bottom of her foot red.

"You need to get this looked at by someone who knows what they're doing. I have no clue how to clean a wound, but that looks seriously messed up." Lauren said.

"It hurts like hell, too. Can you wrap it up again? I'm not sure there's anything we can do about it right now."

"Are you sure? I can try pouring water on it and wiping any dirt off."

"No, I don't think that would help."

"Okay. Let me go get you some new bandages."

Bianca placed the camera next to her on the log, facing Lauren as she walked toward their tent. Bianca spent the thirty seconds humming while she waited for Lauren. The humming stopped, and the footage went silent, minus the trees rustling in the wind, following the sound of something light dropping onto the log behind the camera.

It took Lauren another three minutes to come out of the tent. "Sorry, I couldn't find them, but here they are." She examined the bandages in her hand. "Daniel packed them into his bag-" She looked up toward Bianca and froze. "Bianca?" She said, confused and worried. She ran over to the camera and grabbed it. She pointed it to where Bianca had been sitting, only she wasn't there, only her clothes.

Exactly as she had been wearing them, Bianca's entire outfit, including her unzipped hoodie, her t-shirt beneath, her blue jeans, her single shoe, and even the sock beneath it, were laid out on the log where Bianca was.

"Wasn't she wearing these?" Lauren asked herself, picking up Bianca's shirt, causing her bra to fall out of the bottom.

Nancy: *What the hell?*

Interviewer: *So, I take it you have no idea what happened to her?*

Nancy: *I've heard rumors. Terrible rumors, but is this really it? She just disappears?*

Interviewer: *It seems that way.*

Nancy: *And why are her clothes still there? That's just so ... bizarre.*

Interviewer: *I'm sure you've heard that she was a suspect in all of these tragedies.*

Nancy: *I've heard, and it's ridiculous.*

Interviewer: *Can you at least see why they would think that? I mean, disappearing from the scene of the crime like this-*

Nancy: *No. Not Bianca. She would never.*

Interviewer: *Perhaps she left her clothing behind to throw police off of her trail.*

Nancy: *No, there's no way. Something happened to her, and I don't think I want to know what that is.*

Interviewer: *Do you recall the prom incident she mentioned before? I did some digging, and ... it turns out she was present for another mysterious tragedy, that bears a shocking resemblance to this one. Right after that, she moved back to California and went on this trip with you.*

Nancy: *That sounds awful. Poor girl.*

Interviewer: *That doesn't shock you at all?*

Nancy: *Of course it does! For her to go through something like this twice? I couldn't imagine. And, before you ask, no. I don't think she had something to do with **either** of these events.*

Interviewer: *Fair enough.*

"Bianca?" Lauren yelled. She dropped her shirt and ran behind Mitch's tent, which was the closest. "Bianca, if you're using the bathroom, let me know!"

There was no response.

Lauren took a deep inhale and yelled Bianca's name once more. She ran behind Michael and Nancy's tent. "Why would you take your clothes off?" She screamed, but Bianca was still nowhere to be seen. "Is this another joke? This "bad girl" flirting with me is getting out of hand." She began to walk into the woods. "I don't think you should be walking on that foot!"

The camera pointed toward bushes that were moving.

"Seriously, Bianca. You're taking this way too far. You need to rest until help gets here." She brought the camera to the bush, and she wasn't there. "Oh my gosh, you guys! Are you all in on this? Was this whole thing just one big joke?" She followed more sounds that resembled an animal moving in the woods, like leaves crunching, bushes shaking, and twigs cracking. "Did you all plan on getting me alone in the woods to scare me? Because it's not working!" She yelled.

The footsteps stopped, and Lauren stopped with them. She focused the camera on a tree about six feet from where she stood. "I got you." She whispered. She tiptoed to the tree and waited a second behind it before jumping around the corner for a surprise. "Got you!" She yelled at the figure waiting behind the tree. Only, when she surely expected to catch a scared face on the camera, she was merely at stomach level of the figure. It was the same animal that attacked Mitch and Daniel, large with brown fur. Before Lauren could raise the camera high enough to face it, it lifted its blood-stained arm and grabbed her. The camera lifted with Lauren as she was carried off of the ground by the beast's hand. The footage panned high enough to catch the beast's chest had less fur than the rest of its body, and it looked similar to a male human's.

Before the footage could go any higher, Lauren dropped the camera to the floor, showing the surrounding wilderness while Lauren choked. She tried to scream, but the squeezing on her throat wouldn't allow much more than tiny squeals to come past her gurgling. The sound of her neck snapping followed Lauren's lifeless body, dropping onto the ground in front of the camera

Nancy: *Fuck!*

Interviewer: *Are you okay?*

Nancy: *No, I'm not okay! That was **horrifying**. Lauren was the best of us, and she got it the worst! She did not deserve that. Not that any of them did, but ... you get it.*

Interviewer: *I get it. I'm sorry that you had to see that.*

Nancy: *See it, hear it, the whole thing. Just ... horrible..*

Chapter 14

It's Gonna Be a Long Ride Home

Camera 4

Winston's camera remained on the older man's tent floor for half an hour before the entrance flaps opened again.

"Hello?" Nancy peeked in and ducked so she could step through the entrance. She noticed the man's clothes that were sprawled out on the floor. "Whose tent is this? Oh, no way!" The man's bucket hat he had been wearing when they met him at the gas station was on top of his pillow in the corner behind his wrinkled sleeping bag. She picked it up and started inspecting it. "So it really was him! He was here this whole time!" She put his hat back where it was and scanned the rest of the tent. She noticed the camera. "What?"

She picked up the camera. "Isn't this Winston's? But how could he ... Oh my God." Nancy sounded frightened.

Interviewer: *Can I get some insight into what was going through your head here?*

Nancy: *Well, all we knew was that somebody tried to set our camp on fire and later destroyed our stuff. Then finding my missing friend's camera in the tent solidified the idea that something terrible had happened to them and he had done it. On top of that, I was in the guy's tent. I didn't know if he would be coming back any time soon or not. I was scared for my life, Michael's life ... all of us.*

Nancy picked up a black and white notebook and held it in front of the camera. She opened it slowly with her left hand, holding the camera in her right. She turned through the pages rather quickly, most of them being ineligible notes and scribbles. She turned to a page that read "I WARNED THEM" in red ink across the whole page and something slipped out of the notebook from the back.

Nancy pointed the camera to the item on the floor. It was a Polaroid photo. She picked it up and held it in front of the camera. It was a picture of Nancy's group sitting around the campfire on the first night. "He was spying on us?" She put the photo in her pocket and started going through his belongings, throwing his clothes around, moving his sleeping bag over, and finally discovering a small shoe box beneath a sweater. She opened it, and within were more Polaroids. She scanned a half-dozen of them involving her friends at their campsite. She vocalized her disgust when she came across the photos of them nude at the lake, and she paused when she came across the final picture in the box.

"There's no way." In the photo, clear as day, just as rumored and described, Bigfoot. The creature was tall, had brown fur, stood on two feet, was muscular, and looked terrifying. Not only that, it was in clear view of Nancy and her friends just inside the trees on the opposite side of the lake. "This has got to be a fake right?" She flipped the photo back and forth, looking for any signs of it being fake, and there were none.

Indistinct noises sounded behind the camera, and Nancy dropped the photos she held. "Shit!" She yelled. She grabbed what photos she could, fit them back into the shoe box, and peeked outside the tent. Nobody was there, so she exited the tent and left for the woods.

She traveled about fifty yards before the distant sounds became more precise. They were voices. She followed them once she decided it wasn't coming from the old man, and she ran into two male police officers.

"One of them is still alive." The younger-looking one said into his walkie-talkie.

"Still alive? What do you mean?" Nancy asked.

"It's okay. You're safe." The younger one said.

"Ma'am, what is your name?" The older one said.

"My name is Nancy. Where are my friends?" Nancy asked.

"You were here with that group, right? Your friend Alyssa brought us here to find you." The older officer said.

"Yes, I'm with them! Where the fuck are my friends? What did you mean still alive?"

"Just come with us back to camp, please. We will talk as soon as we get out of here."

***

Camera 3

Alyssa arrived back at the camp with a caravan of police and ambulance following behind her. When she got out of her car, she noticed that the camp was empty, and the police quickly dispersed into the woods to find her friends. Over the next hour, Alyssa filmed her own hell-on-earth experience as she would describe it to an officer later, as they, one after the other, brought her friend's corpses out of the woods in body bags, counting four in total.

The police would not let her see the bodies, simply saying, "You don't want to see them like this."

In a bright change of pace, she would run to Mitch's side as they pulled him out, not in a bag but on a stretcher. She pointed the camera to his leg that the animal had chewed at the thigh through to the bone. "What happened?" She asked.

"Alyssa." He smiled at her. He reached into his pocket and pulled out the ring he was showing Daniel before his attack. "Will you marry me?"

"Oh, Mitch!" She let out a single laugh through her tears. "Yes!" She reached her hand out so he could place the ring on her, but the paramedics began to lift him into the ambulance.

"I'm sorry, miss, but we need to take him now if he's going to make it." A female paramedic said.

"Of course." She said. She filmed them closing the doors behind Mitch and driving away. She brought the camera to the campsite and took notice of Bianca's clothes on the log but did not say anything. She sat and cried silently, waiting for more of her friends to come out of the woods.

The last one for them to bring out was Nancy. She held her camera down on one side and the shoe box on the other. She appeared defeated.

"Nancy!" Alyssa yelled and ran to her. They hugged and cried together.

"What happened? Where is everybody?" Nancy asked after some stuttering.

"I … I don't know."

Alyssa filmed Nancy while she was pulled away by a couple of officers to have the situation explained to her. She recorded the exact moment that Nancy understood that their friends had died.

Nancy's legs went limp, and she fell to the floor. She screamed with her hands in her face to catch the tears.

Alyssa tried to approach and comfort her, but she had broken down herself.

The police tried telling them that it might be best to leave the woods while they looked for their final friend, Bianca, but they insisted on staying and waiting. Hours went by, and it started to get dark.

Finally, an officer approached them and advised that they would continue the search overnight, but it was unsafe for them to stay. They would have to assign an officer to protect them at the campsite. An officer that could otherwise be used to look for the friend.

Nancy and Alyssa agreed that they would leave. Nancy suggested they stay in a hotel, but Alyssa would go to the hospital to be with Mitch.

An officer whose shift was coming close to ending offered them a ride to the hospital, and they took it.

As they walked to the car, Alyssa asked Nancy, "What's with the shoe box?"

"You wouldn't believe it if you saw it," Nancy said but showed her regardless. She opened the box and handed Alyssa the photo of them at the lake with Bigfoot in the background.

"Oh my God! Is this real?" Alyssa asked when they got into the car.

"I'm not sure," Nancy said.

The cop got in after them and started driving away.

"Where did you find this?" Alyssa asked.

"That crazy old guy from the gas station? He had a tent in the woods. He was watching us." Nancy handed Alyssa the shoe box.

The cop overheard and questioned Nancy about the guy that was watching them. He made it evident that this man was a clear-cut suspect in the murder of their friends, but Alyssa and Nancy voiced their doubts due to the injuries the paramedics described to them.

When Alyssa finally shut off the camera, "I'm Still Standing" by Elton John was playing through the car's speakers.

Chapter 15

Closing Interview

"It's all over," The interviewer said.

Nancy's face was red and moist with tears. She sniffled and wiped her eyes.

"I'm sorry you had to see all of that again."

"It's for the best," Nancy said.

"Do you need any break before we go on to our final round of questions?"

"No, but can I get some water, please?"

"Of course."

An intern of the film crew popped into the frame to hand Nancy a bottle.

"Thank you." She said. "What did you want to ask?" She twisted the cap open and took a sip.

"I'm sure the answer is an obvious one, but how do you feel right now? Does it feel like there's any weight off your chest? Did you have any pleasant memories brought back from this experience?"

"A weight off my chest is hard to say, but I think it might fit. Maybe if you asked me tomorrow, I could say for certain. Right now, I'm just overwhelmed. As for pleasant memories, oh yes.

There were plenty. Seeing my old friends having fun again was hard, knowing what had happened, but I felt like I was right there with them again. That is a feeling that I've missed for a long time."

"I'm glad to hear it. I was worried that this whole thing would be too much for you. I know I couldn't handle it, but I think you've done well. I'm envious of your resolve."

"Thank you."

"So, for this next part, I'm going to go through a list of your friends, and I just want to have a small discussion about them. Feel free to say anything you like or nothing at all. And remember, we can stop this at any time."

"Go for it." She sighed.

"Okay, Winston. Tell me, how does it feel having finally seen what he went through?"

"It was tough. Winston wasn't my closest friend, but I do miss him. We took his presence for granted and didn't deserve him."

"How about Lauren?"

"She seemed like she was really coming into her own. She was a good friend, and I was so happy to see her coming out of her cage and enjoying life. It's such a shame that this tragedy ripped the experience away from her so soon. I wish I had reached out to her family more after all of this, but I just felt so guilty for having her join us in the first place. They're such nice people that I know they wouldn't ever blame me for what happened, but I couldn't face them after that."

"I'm sorry to hear that. Next on the list is Daniel."

"Daniel and I were never that close, to begin with, but it was hard seeing him again. We got to know each other on this trip, which was a lot of fun. He would've grown to be a fine husband and father to a lucky woman one day, and I know that his father would've been so proud of him."

"I'm sure he would have. Now, this will be a little more of a direct question. What is your opinion on what happened to Bianca? I'm sure you know that they never found her body."

"Yeah, I've heard all of the bullshit. People think that Bianca had something to do with their murders. I get that it's suspicious, but the type of wounds that my friends suffered was far too much for any person to do! Look, I'm not sure what happened to her. It is weird. It was probably the weirdest thing to happen on the trip, but she didn't have anything to do with their deaths. She had to have died out there with the rest of them. If she were still alive, she would have approached me by now. Someone would have noticed her. I hate to say it, but she's gone."

"Fair enough. Now, for the last one on this list, Michael."

"Oh, boy," Nancy said, wiping a tear from her eye and laughing.

"So, you've voiced your opinion on him being a dick throughout this documentary, and forgive me if I'm overstepping, but I couldn't help but notice you were smiling at the good times during these tapes and how upset it made you during his final moments. Why don't you provide a little insight into your emotions that you went through, watching him and your relationship with him during its final moments?"

Nancy tried to speak but struggled. She tried to hold back her tears, but that only made them come through stronger. She wiped her nose off on her wrist and sniffled.

"Someone get her a tissue, please." The interviewer said.

The intern again entered the frame and handed her a box of tissues.

"Thank you." She said. "My relationship with Michael was a complicated one." She sniffled once again before wiping her eyes. "The truth is, I miss him. I really do. We had our problems. Every relationship does. And he had his anger issues that made him an asshole, but I loved him. Honestly, I am just mad at him. I think I mentally had to blame *someone* for what we all went through that week, and every time I went to point a finger, it pointed at Michael. He was the one that brought us out there, he was the one that made us stay, and he was the one that left me alone. Everything made me think it was his fault, but it wasn't. He didn't know what would happen, and this process has helped me realize that."

"I'm sorry."

"Don't be. Thank you."

"For what?"

"For asking about him. It's a tough question to ask someone in my position, but I respect you for taking the chance. Without answering a question like that, I don't know if I ever would've admitted how I felt about him, and I don't know if I ever would've forgiven him."

"So do you? Forgive him?"

"Yes. I do."

"I'm glad … Before I get you out of here, I want to ask about you. How has your life been since this tragedy."

"It's been awful. I regret most of it. I feel sorry that I got to live and *they didn't*. I feel undeserving. I've tried to move on, but it doesn't work. I've tried to see other people, but they all suck. They either know what I've gone through and see me as some item of their fantasy, to feel close to Bigfoot, or they leave me as soon as they find out I'm a complete wreck. I would even scare away any one-night stands because I would wake them up screaming from night terrors. I did find one guy that was special. I'm not going to name him here because I don't want to ruin *his* life by flooding it with paparazzi, but that relationship ended even more tragically than the rest. He understood me for what I went through and did his best to make me feel safe and loved. We got pregnant and engaged, and I *almost* felt happy. However, as the doctor would put it, with the amount of anxiety my body and mind were constantly under, there was no way I could carry the child to term. I ended up miscarrying, and *he* left soon after. I don't blame him. I was even more of a wreck after we lost the baby, and he couldn't be around me. He needed to mourn on his own. Everything I touch dies. At least, that's how I feel. I'm hoping that it will all get better after this."

"Wow, that's … really sad. I don't know what to say."

"You don't have to say anything."

"At the very least, let me say that I hope things get better for you."

"Thank you."

"Lastly, we have a bit of a surprise for you."

"You didn't have to do anything like that."

"Of course we did. We are here to get you closure, and I think this might help. If you noticed, the two friends we haven't asked about, Mitch and Alyssa-"

"Oh, no."

"We are aware of the fact that you guys haven't been entirely close since the tragedy. We contacted them on getting involved with the documentary, and they said that they wouldn't be capable of going through with the watching of the footage-"

"You didn't." Nancy seemed worried.

"Yes, we did. We invited both of them to come out and reconnect with you. They are actually here now."

"Both of them? Together? I didn't think it possible after their divorce."

"We weren't sure about it either, but they're here. I'm sorry that we are throwing this on you, but with your permission, we would like to invite them inside and-"

The door behind Nancy opened, and she turned around. She covered her mouth in shock as she saw Alyssa pushing Mitch into the room in his wheelchair.

His injured leg was missing from the hip.

"Oh my God." Nancy jumped out of her seat and held out her arms for a hug, bending down to hug Mitch first.

"I'd stand for you if I could." He said, returning the hug.

Nancy released him to hug Alyssa next. "It's so good to see you guys."

"It's so good to see you, too," Alyssa said.

Tears started to form in all three of their eyes.

"I don't want to interrupt this, but why don't we get you guys some seats and ask the three of you some questions while you all reconnect." The interviewer said.

"Thanks for the offer, but I've already got my seat," Mitch said.

Nancy giggled.

"That would be great, thank you."

***

The three of them sat in the camera's frame.

"Now, the three of you have had the opportunity to see each other again. How does it feel?" The interviewer asked.

"Surreal," Nancy said. "Seriously, how are you guys? I heard about the divorce."

"Oh, we are fine. At least, we are now." Mitch said.

"Things were tough for a while, but we are in a better place," Alyssa said.

"What happened? If you don't mind me asking." Nancy asked.

"It's hard to say," Mitch said.

"Yeah. I think after so many years, we just forgot who we were. We started fighting a lot, and it just became unbearable. For the both of us." Alyssa said.

"Oh my gosh, I'm sorry to hear that. I have to ask! How is the kid? Were they upset when you divorced?" Nancy asked.

"She's not so much a kid anymore. She has one of her own now."

"No way!" Nancy said.

"Yeah, and our little grandbaby is turning eighteen next month," Alyssa said.

Nancy's jaw fell to the floor. She started to cry. "I'm sorry I haven't been around."

"Don't be. We understand." Mitch said.

"Of course you do. You always do! But that doesn't make it right. I just ... it was hard. Whenever I tried to reach out, I would think about that trip. That cursed trip. I couldn't handle it. Instead, I did my best to forget. I'm sorry that meant cutting you out and missing out on your child's life. I'm really, *really* sorry." Nancy's crying became worse.

"It's okay, really. Trust me, it was hard for us, too. We all went through our own trauma during that trip. Perhaps that's what ended up tearing Mitch and I apart. Nobody could be mentally healthy after what we went through." Alyssa said.

"You're right. I'm sorry, just ... excuse me." Nancy took a tissue and rubbed her eye as she left the room.

"Poor girl," Mitch said.

"She's going through a lot, as I'm sure you would understand. It's been a long couple of days." The interviewer said.

"So she did it, then?" Alyssa asked.

"She watched the tapes?" Mitch said.

"She did."

"Wow. She's doing better than I ever could." Alyssa said and shook her head, almost as if she had a spasm.

"So, while I have the two of you here, why don't I ask about you guys? How are you doing? You mentioned being in a better place now. What does that mean?"

"We sort of … reconnected," Alyssa said.

"We hooked up," Mitch said.

Alyssa backhanded his shoulder. "That's not what I meant."

"Oh! Right. Yeah, she called me soon after you guys did. We reconnected." Mitch said.

"We talked over dinner about coming together for this documentary and started reliving some of our good times. We decided to forget about anything we've gone through in the past and try to work on fixing our relationship. Even if that means just being friendly, if not for us, than for a better life for our family." Alyssa said.

"Only it happened to be a little more than friendly very quickly," Mitch said.

Alyssa shook her head in disappointment.

"Alright then." The interviewer laughed. "Tell me about your grandkid. How are they doing?"

"Oh, she's great," Alyssa said.

"Yeah, she will be working for me this Summer."

Alyssa looked at him like this was the first time she had been hearing this.

Nancy walked back into the room. "Sorry, I had to use the restroom really quickly." She took her seat. "What is it that you do? Last I checked, you were opening some sort of camp, right?"

"Exactly. A few years back, I opened a Summer camp for kids who have struggled with various traumas. It's meant to teach them to handle their emotions healthily, communicate with other people who may have gone through similar, and eventually live a better life."

"Wow. That sounds like something I could've used." Nancy said.

"That sounds amazing." The interviewer said.

"We all could've used it," Alyssa said.

"Alyssa has her concerns," Mitch said.

"Of course I do! I don't see how you could send all those kids to the wilderness after what happened to us." Alyssa said. "But, I have to admit that it's been great for those kids, so I won't say any more than that."

"I could see where your concerns are coming from." The interviewer said.

"Yeah, you're crazy for wanting to do *anything* involving the wilderness," Nancy said. "I don't even like the trees in my neighbor's yard."

"Well, maybe you should check it out. Come by, and I will show you the work those kids are doing. Something about it makes me feel special." Mitch said.

"I wish I could say maybe, but I'm not sure I ever could," Nancy said.

"I don't blame you," Alyssa said. "He's tried to get me to go, but I just can't."

"Yeah, I'm not sure," Nancy said.

"If you ever change your mind, I'm not a hard person to reach," Mitch said.

"Well, it has been lovely, everyone. I don't want to keep you all for too much longer. I think it might be best to leave you alone to reconnect by yourselves now, and I don't think there is much more I can ask you. So, before I go, is there anything you three would like to say? Anything to get off your chests? Any final words?" The interviewer asked.

The three of them looked at each other.

"Whether you believe us or not," Nancy said, "Bigfoot is real."

"If you go into the woods, don't go alone. Bring a friend." Alyssa said.

"And a gun." Mitch said.

"Stay safe out there." Nancy said, and the others nodded.

The camera faded to black.

Also by Matthew Mercer

It Came From Above

Mysterious disappearances. A helpless group of friends. Will any of them survive?

Sean finally has an opportunity to take his long time crush Samantha on a date. They go to the drive-in movie theater, they're flirting back and forth, and everything is going perfectly. That is, until she disappears.

In this story, reminiscent of classic 80s slasher films, Sean and his friends try their best at finding out what really happened that night, while trying to avoid meeting their own demise along the way.

It Came From the Loch

It has been over two decades since Elizabeth lost her family in a tragic event on Loch Ness.

Now, in a half-work-half-vacation, she is making her return with Alexa, her partner from work, Hailey, her seven-year-old daughter, and Brooke and Marcus, her friends from college, to study an influx of sea turtles that found their way into Loch Ness and hopefully find some answers about actually what happened to her family in the process.

Things soon go South once a stewardess goes missing on the loch, and Elizabeth finds herself reliving her childhood nightmare.

Notes From the Author

Coming off of my first book, I told myself that I needed to use my next one to focus on perfecting character development. I still have a long way to go, but this book helped me become a lot more comfortable in bringing my characters to life and giving them their own personalities.

This book was a lot of fun for me, and a big part of that was the challenge I gave myself with my narrative style. I am a huge fan of found-footage horror. Paranormal Activity was one of the first movies that truly frightened me growing up, and I wanted to see how I could mix that formula with the slasher one. It was much more complicated than I realized, but I am so proud of the outcome once everything came together.

My next book, It Came From the Loch, will be the last in the "It Came" series for a short time while I work on my first full-length novel. I won't give any more information on that just yet, but I promise it will be great.

If you were a fan of this book, my last one, or anything I release from here on out, please follow me on any of my social media platforms. I have a blog I'm working on keeping active on my website: AspectsEntertainment.com, where I discuss my projects and review horror movies and books. You can also follow Aspects Entertainment, my publishing company, on Facebook, Instagram, Twitter, TikTok, and YouTube. Every follow helps, and I appreciate all of you.

Thank you for reading.

Keep reading for a sneak peek.

Prologue

I t was a cold spring night out on the water. The breeze blew gracefully across young Elizabeth's scalp. She stared outward, between the deck's guardrails, at the reflection of the moon bouncing off the water. She closed her eyes and listened for the sounds of nature. She picked up the waves crashing against the yacht, birds chirping overhead, the American flag flapping with the wind, and alcoholic laughter from the dining hall behind her.

She came out to the deck to escape the party and noise. Her family often overwhelmed her, and she liked isolating herself to calm her nerves. She understood they were on vacation, so she couldn't be mad at them, but she had dealt with enough of their drinking at home to develop a hatred for it. However, being alone on a large body of water like this was much more exciting than her usual hiding place in her room.

At least, it *was* until her cousin Bradley stumbled his way onto the deck beside her.

Elizabeth could list her problems with alcohol for days; the smell it left on their breath, the sticky sweat that would paint itself on consumers' foreheads, the bottomless pit it left in her parents' wallets, etc., but her biggest problem was how much it followed her. To her, no matter how much she avoided it, ran from it, hid from it, alcohol would find its way to get to her. For example, right now. Here she was, letting the adults have their fun, trying to get away from it all and enjoy nature, and out comes her least favorite cousin.

She only had three cousins. First, there is Bradley, her oldest cousin, the son of Roger, her mother's brother. Then, Jamie and James were the twin siblings from her Aunt Christie on her father's side.

She wasn't very close to any of them, but Bradley was her least favorite because he was the most inappropriate. She didn't think he meant any harm, but she was never entirely comfortable around him.

Her parents would always excuse his poor behavior with a simple, "Don't mind him, he's drunk," but the bigger problem was that he was *always* drunk.

It took longer than it should have for him to get to the edge of the deck where she sat, the rocking of the boat didn't help his drunken knees, and he didn't seem to notice that she was even there.

This didn't surprise Elizabeth. She was only eight years old and, therefore, tiny. On top of that, she understood that his vision probably wasn't great through all the drinking. Elizabeth was very bright for her age. She tried extra hard in school to learn what she could and spent a lot of time learning to be independent, living in a house with alcoholic parents. She often felt embarrassed of them and over-compensated with her learning so she could *feel* like she was better than they were in some way. However, all of the knowledge in the world could not have prepared her for what Bradley would do next.

He stood next to her, his hip bone less than a foot away from her temple, unzipped his pants, placed his penis on the railing, and exhaled when he let out his hands-free piss stream.

She forced herself to look away. She closed her eyes and imagined the moon's reflection in the water in an attempt not to let that image of him burn into her memory.

"You're missing one *hell* of a party in there, girly," Bradley said as he shook out the last drops of urine.

So, he did know I was here? Elizabeth was preparing a response but lost it as a drop landed on her cheek. She had dealt with many disgusting things in her short life, but that moment shot right up to the top of her list. Her jaw would've fallen to the floor if she weren't afraid of catching another drop, this time on her tongue. The voice of her parents saying, "he's just drunk," echoed around in her head, but it didn't help her. Nothing could. She waited for the sound of his pants zipping back up to face him.

He bent down, placing his hands on his knees to bring his head to her height. "How about I sneak you out some whiskey? It's pretty cold out here tonight. I'm sure that will warm you right up."

"Leave that little girl alone." Another man called from the dining room's entrance. It was her Uncle Roger, her favorite of her relatives.

"I'm just trying to cheer her up."

"I don't care what you're doing," Bradley's father interrupted. "Get back in there and enjoy the party. Us sober folks need some time alone."

This was why he was her favorite. He hadn't always been, but for as long as she could remember, he was the sober one. Around the time she was born, alcohol poisoning hospitalized him. She heard from members of the family that he had a severe problem with drinking, in contrast to what they called their "social drinking." She would always roll her eyes at the thought. Either way, it *was* true that it had hospitalized him, and he was on the verge of liver failure, so there *must* have been some truth to the story. He had a severe change in luck once he got out of the hospital, so severe that she always pictured him getting whiplash from the events.

Once he could leave his house without assistance from another person, he found himself at the liquor store. He didn't have much left in his wallet, but he planned on using it to drink himself to sleep that night. Instead, he saw the sign for a lottery ticket in the window above the store's entrance. He thought about it and made himself a promise. He would spend the last of his money on a chance for a better future. If that opportunity came through, he would take it. And he did. The lottery ticket was a winner. Elizabeth wasn't sure of the amount, only that it was in the nine digits. Roger took it as a sign from *something* telling him to fix his life, and he chose never to drink again. He would have his struggles, first at big family events, then eventually at home once Bradley started to drink. Being around others that drink made it hard for a recovering alcoholic not to. He took his money and moved to Scotland, leaving his adult son behind with his ex-wife, leaving the rest of his family and life that he had built in America, and focused on sobriety.

Elizabeth had gotten to know him after a few years had passed, and he was confident enough in himself to fly to family functions and be in that environment without grabbing a bottle. Elizabeth always loved when he came around because he would be the only family member that wouldn't stumble over drunken words. She could hold an actual conversation with him and remember it the next day. He made her feel safe.

That brings us to today. Roger wanted to celebrate five full years of sobriety by inviting his entire family to see his home, an expensive hillside mansion overlooking Loch Ness. He paid for their flights and promised to keep them all fed during their stay.

Now, Elizabeth was here with more of her family than she had ever met while they celebrated on the loch aboard her uncle's yacht.

Bradley looked back at her. His breath was visible as it traveled warmly through the cold air to her face.

She hated the smell of it.

"Don't have to tell me twice." Bradley stood upright and walked as straight as he could to the dining room.

"That son of mine." Roger shook his head and sat down beside her. "He didn't bother you too much, did he?"

Elizabeth shook her head, "no," in her best attempt to seem strong. She couldn't hold back her instinct to rub her face onto her bicep, hoping that all of her cousin's bladder fluids were gone.

The boat rocked beneath them, this time more aggressive than it usually would against the waves, but they didn't pay it any mind.

"Are you having fun out here? In Scotland, I mean." Roger asked.

Elizabeth nodded, "yes."

"This is probably your first time out of the country, isn't it? What do you think?"

"The people here talk funny!" Elizabeth said.

"They do, don't they?" Roger chuckled. "Don't go telling that to their faces." He shook his hand through her hair, making a mess of it. He looked back out toward the water. "It's beautiful, isn't it?"

She looked in the same direction he did, really taking in the sight this time. "Mesmerizing," she said. It was a new word to her, and she was excited to use it.

"There she is!" Her mother's voice called from behind them.

"Are you enjoying the lake out here, Lizzy?" Her father, Jared, followed.

"It's called a loch!" Elizabeth said.

Her parents shared looks of amusement.

"She's right, you know?" Roger said. "Loch Ness."

"Well, *excuse* us!" Her mother said playfully.

"Are you enjoying *Loch Ness*, Elizabeth?" Her father said.

"It's beautiful."

"It is, isn't it?" Her mother said.

Elizabeth was impressed with how composed the two of them were. She figured they would both be plastered by this time tonight. She figured her father's tie would be undone, his upper buttons would have been unbuttoned, and her mother's heels would have come off by now. She assumed they would have found their way to their bedroom below deck and fallen asleep, forgetting about their daughter, their only responsibility. She wasn't wrong to have the assumptions because they all come from past experiences, but she was disappointed in herself for thinking so negatively of her parents.

"I think we are going to call it an early night tonight. Most of the others are finding their way to their rooms if they haven't already passed out at their tables, and we have to get up early enough to prep for our flight home. Why don't you come inside and say good night to everyone before we go to bed?" Her mother reached her hand out to pick up Elizabeth.

"Nonsense, Monica. Who knows how long it will take until she gets to come back here again? I'm not always going to be able to pay for everybody's flights. Let her stay out with me for a little while longer. I'll make sure she gets to your room safely." Roger said.

Monica looked at her husband as if she was asking for his approval for her brother's idea.

"That should be fine. But not too late." He raised his finger, pretending to be stern with him, but he laughed it off and took his wife by the arm and led her downstairs. The yacht shook aggressively again, causing the married couple to grip the handrail with white knuckles to stop themselves from falling.

"Are you guys okay?" Roger asked them.

Elizabeth's father responded with a simple thumbs-up and continued down the steps.

"Is the boat supposed to shake like that?" Elizabeth asked.

"Of course it is!" Roger said, but his face didn't seem so sure. "It's just what happens when the waves decide to push us around."

"But, that badly?"

"Waves are like people," Roger said.

Elizabeth tilted her head in curiosity.

"They aren't all the same size. For example, you are tiny. I am rather normal-sized, at least I'd like to say so. Then, there's your

Aunt Christie. She would be one of the waves causing the boat to shake like that," Roger said with a smile.

Elizabeth broke into laughter. Her Aunt Christie was a lovely lady, but she was often on the butt-end of many heavy-set jokes from her Uncle Roger. She overheard him say a joke about her one Thanksgiving, and he's been making them ever since he saw the way it made her laugh.

The laughing didn't go on for much longer as another shaking of the yacht occurred, this time more violent than the rest.

Elizabeth and her Uncle lost their balance in their seats on the floor, Elizabeth falling backward hard enough to slam her head onto the wooden deck floor. If the ringing in her ears wasn't already enough noise for her new headache, her drunken family's screaming was.

"That one wasn't your Aunt Christie," Roger said, rubbing his eyes as he sat back up. "Shit, Lizzy, are you okay?"

Elizabeth prepared to nod, but the yacht shook again, with a voluminous thud between a surge of water splashing against the boat's right side, rocking them again.

"Get inside!" Roger yelled, struggling to stand to his feet.

Elizabeth got up from the ground and started to move toward the dining hall, looking back to ensure her uncle was on his feet.

He was. Only, he wasn't following her. Instead, he leaned over the boat's guardrail, looking for what was causing the ruckus.

"Do you see something?" Elizabeth's aunt, Tabitha, asked from the upper deck above the dining room.

"Nothing at all!" Roger saw that Elizabeth was still waiting for him in the doorway outside of the dining room. "Get inside!

What are you doing?" He pointed to the door behind her and ran across the deck to the other side to peer over the edge.

The hit, whatever it was, came from the back of the yacht this time, knocking it upwards at a steep enough angle to knock Tabitha over the railing, where she fell almost twenty feet onto the deck below, landing on her neck in front of Elizabeth.

Elizabeth screamed while her uncle watched in terror. He ran to Tabitha's side and yelled at Elizabeth, "Don't look at her! Find your parents."

Elizabeth didn't object. She ran into the dining room, past family members screaming and stampeding in different directions. Some to the stairs on the left, others to the right, and the few who saw Tabitha's fall ran toward Elizabeth so they could check on her. All of them had to step over knocked-over tables and chairs and broken glass from the dishes they had been eating throughout the night.

Elizabeth made it to the stairs on the left side, which she knew to take to her room where her parents were supposed to be. Half a dozen of her family members blocked the stairs, most of which she didn't recognize. At the bottom of the stairs was Jamie, the female of her twin cousins. Her Aunt Christie was attending to her daughter's ankle, which looked swollen. Next to them, Jamie's high heel laid on the floor with a broken heel.

She must have fallen, Elizabeth thought.

Something slammed the side of the ship beside them, splashing water over the railing and drenching everyone near the bottom of the stairs. The family screamed, echoing in the stairwell and filling Elizabeth's young ears with a ringing that she shouldn't have expected for another fifteen years *at least*. Rather than waiting for Jamie and Christie to move out of the way, they stormed over them, not all of them clearing them without trampling them. Elizabeth noticed more than one person stepping directly onto Jamie's injured ankle, but nobody cared. They couldn't.

Elizabeth was scared herself, but she was small enough to squeak past them without further injury once the rest of the family had cleared the walkway. She ran as fast as her little legs could to the back of the yacht where her room was, slipping once on the wet floor along the way. She swung the door open and found her parents inside. Her father was on the floor, his right leg pinned beneath an eight-drawer, vertical dresser that must have fallen over from an instance of the boat shaking.

Her mother was struggling to lift the dresser off of him. She turned around once Elizabeth entered the room and looked as relieved as she could in the moment. "Oh, honey, you're okay! Thank God. Please, come help me lift this. I just need a little more room."

Without question, Elizabeth ran to the top end of the dresser while her mom lifted it from the side. Elizabeth put both hands on the back and used all of her body's strength, her feet sliding on the carpet as she pushed.

Her mother grunted, and her father screamed in pain, but once his leg was free enough to move, he slipped out from underneath, and both girls dropped the dresser. It slammed as loud as the carpet would let it, and her mother rushed to his side, where he leaned against the bed's footboard.

"What the *fuck* is happening?" He asked.

"We need to make sure everyone else is okay," Monica said.

Elizabeth wanted to object, she felt safer inside, but before they could even get up from the floor, something slammed into the boat again. This time, it was met with the sounds of metal screeching and glass shattering.

Elizabeth's parents took her by the hand and escorted her out of the room. They went around the back corner of where the rooms were aligned, toward the direct back of the boat, where there was another set of stairs. Only, this time, there wasn't.

They had to come to a screeching halt, her mother losing her footing on the wet wooden boards and slipping just inches away from the giant hole in the floor that they saw for the first time, her heels falling off her feet and into the water below. Everything was gone from the railing, the walkway, and the wall. They could see into the floor below, filled with storage boxes of alcohol and fresh produce ingredients. They could also see into the empty bedroom that was now soaked on the inside and missing the same dresser that every room had, the one identical in style to the one that had fallen on Elizabeth's father.

"Did we hit something?" He asked, lifting his wife to her feet.

"There's nothing here!" She yelled.

"Where's your brother?" He asked.

"He's probably still at the front deck," Elizabeth said.

"Shit!" Her father said, looking into the room below.

Elizabeth leaned her head as far as she felt comfortable. She could see the water begin to fill the room.

"The boat is going to sink," Monica said.

"Come on. We have to go tell everyone else." Her father took both of them by the hands and ran them back down the walkway Elizabeth had run by herself. "We're sinking!" He yelled as he ran.

Elizabeth could hear her family gasping through their open bedroom doors and asking what had happened as they ran past. They made it up the stairs, Jamie and Christie no longer blocking the way, and went upstairs.

Inside the dining room, Roger sat with James, the male twin. They both seemed devastated, and Elizabeth knew why once she saw Tabitha outside the dining room's entrance door, covered in a white tablecloth. She had died.

"What happened?" Monica asked. Her fear had turned to confusion.

"I'm sorry. I couldn't help her." James said.

"No, it's not your fault." Roger's voice cracked as he put his hand on his shoulder.

"What, who is it?" Monica asked

"Aunt Tabitha," Elizabeth said.

Monica looked at her daughter with her eyebrows narrowed, then back to her brother. She realized that it was true by the look on Roger's face. "What? No...." She gasped and looked back at Elizabeth, "And you saw? Oh my...." Monica looked at her daughter while her eyes filled with tears. She started to run, but Roger yelled.

"Don't!"

Monica stopped.

"It isn't pretty. Just ... don't," he said.

Monica fell to her knees, but it didn't last long as the boat started to rise from its front end.

"I'm sorry, but we don't have time," Jared said.

Roger and James stood up, holding their hands at awkward angles like it was helping them balance.

"There is a big hole in the back of the ship. It is filling with water, and we are going to sink soon. We need to get off the ship." Jared said.

Elizabeth admired how calm her father was in this situation. She took extra notice of how happy she was that he seemed sober enough to make this situation less scary for everyone else involved.

Roger nodded and helped Jared lift Monica. They made their way outside to the front of the boat, where most of the family ran from every different direction. Everyone was a mess. They were all confused and scared, some screaming, most asking what was happening. None of them had answers.

They all leaned over the front handrail and looked into the water for an answer. To their shock, they finally saw something. A shadow. It was hard to determine a shape. It was dark outside, and the water was darker, but undeniably, something was moving below them, and that something was big.

If they didn't have enough problems, the boat was hit again, this time directly in the center of the ship. To make matters worse, the boat had split horizontally from one end to the other.

"Grab the ledge!" Roger yelled.

Elizabeth listened, but not everyone else did. Both halves of the ship were lifting from opposite ends, slowly morphing into a v-shape in the water. Elizabeth heard her family screaming as they slid down the dock toward the water. She was too scared to look behind her, telling herself:

Don't look down.

She listened to her own advice until she saw James' fingers slipping on the railing to her right. She couldn't help but keep her eyes on him when he fell, but he didn't fall into the water. He slammed into the glass window of the dining room, shattering it and disappearing deeper into the ship.

"Pull me up!" Monica yelled.

Elizabeth looked to her left side now, where her father was hanging from the rail, and her mother was hanging onto his ankle, dangling beneath him. The boat's front end was pointing straight toward the moon above them. Her mother hung parallel to the floor.

"I'm trying!" Jared yelled, lifting his knee as high as he could, but he was his wife's weight pulling at his injured leg caused too much pain for him to handle.

"Mommy!" Elizabeth yelled, and everything froze around her. Or, at least, that's how it felt when her dad lost his grip on the railing, and both of her parents descended in what felt like slow motion into the water below. Elizabeth couldn't scream. She couldn't move a muscle. The whole world went dark, and she felt numb. She hung there for an eternity, waiting for her parents to emerge from the water.

She got her hopes up when she saw *something* coming up, but it wasn't them. It was both her aunt Christie and her cousin Jamie, and they were dead. She felt like she was sinking herself, living an actual nightmare, and it took her Uncle Roger, hanging from the same railing behind where her parents were, to bring her back down to earth.

"Elizabeth!" He yelled, snapping her out of her trance. "Your parents will be *fine*. But I need you to listen to me. Are you listening?"

Elizabeth nodded but kept bringing her eyes away from him to look down for her parents.

"I need you to hang on. Don't let go no matter what, you hear me? Quit looking down there. Look up, and focus. You must hold onto this railing until your feet touch the water. When they do, let go and swim to shore. Do you understand?" He said.

Elizabeth swallowed her fear and nodded.

"Say it!" He said.

"I understand." She said.

"Okay, close your eyes if you need to, but do *not* look down there."

"Okay." She said and looked forward to the deck floor. "I'm scared."

"I know, sweetie. Me, too. But you will be okay. I promise," He said.

Elizabeth closed her eyes and started counting. It was how she would calm herself when she was stressed, and it was how she often fell asleep when her parents were drunk and loud outside her bedroom door on most nights. Only, this time, she didn't wish for better parents. She didn't wish for a happy family like she often would. She didn't wish for a better life. She wished only for *her* parents' safety. She wished for *her* life to be the same a week from now as it was before this trip. She focused on her wishes and tried to picture her life as a happy one, ignoring the screams of her family in the water from the opposite end of the boat. She heard water splashing to her left side.

"Holy shit!" Roger yelled, followed by even more splashing, this time close to her.

With that splashing came an abundance of water, drenching her backside. She wanted to open her eyes and look, but she focused all her energy on maintaining her grip on the railing, that same grip now covered in freezing-cold water, the only plus side being that the numbness of her hands was better than pain.

Completely unaware of how much time had passed, she finally felt the water climbing up her foot to her ankle. It was time to let go.

She opened her eyes and looked to her left for her uncle. She wanted his approval to jump in the water, primarily because she realized now that she didn't know how to swim. That wasn't her biggest problem, though. No, her problem was that her uncle was gone. She looked all around and could not see any of her family.

The other half of the yacht was now entirely submerged. The water seemed empty behind her, she was a half-mile away from shore, and she was alone.

She continued hanging onto the railing for as long as possible, only letting go once her head fully submerged. She tried to recall every swimming instruction she had ever received, but nothing worked. She waved her arms, kicked her legs, and tried to relax as much as possible. Everything she tried made her sink faster.

She wasn't ready to give up but felt like this was it. She thought it was unfair.

I'm only eight years old, she told herself, *I don't deserve this.*

Her body was now becoming as numb as her fingers were. She thought that fear was an emotion she hadn't gotten to know all too well by now, but this was something else entirely.

She eventually ran out of air and tried to inhale as a reflex. Water from the Loch flooded her throat.

Before entering the yacht, her family had teased her with stories about a monster that lurked beneath the depths. Some prehistoric dinosaur survived all of the world-changing catastrophes, and only a few people have ever spotted it. She didn't buy any of it. She was too bright for that. At least, that was what she thought. But now, she wasn't so sure. What else could have attacked them like this?

She screamed a silent, breathless scream into the water when something wrapped around her waist. She looked down for the monster, but everything below her was black. She couldn't even see her own hands that punched her attacker. However, this didn't hurt like she thought being eaten alive would. It didn't hurt at all! The moonlight reached her head and started filling out her body. Whatever it was, it was bringing her to the surface! She felt herself getting lightheaded from a lack of oxygen.

When she finally emerged from the water, she spit out all the water that filled her mouth and coughed up some more. She took the deepest breath she ever had, and her savior emerged below her.

It was her cousin Bradley. For the first time *ever*, she was happy to see him.

He matched her deep inhale and wiped his hair out of his eyes. "Are you okay?"

Elizabeth kept silent. It was obvious that she wasn't okay. None of this was okay, but she didn't have the proper vocabulary prowess to discuss it with him then.

"Can you swim?" He asked.

She shook her head, "no."

"Okay, I will just have to carry you," he wrapped his arm around her back.

She hugged him tightly and watched their backs as he swam toward shore. She saw as the last of the yacht sunk below the depths of the water.

"I got stuck in the dining room. I was behind that bar when the boat flipped," he said.

Of course, you were, she thought, but she couldn't stay mad at him. Not now. He was all she had left. She turned her head toward the beach they approached and saw the flashing red lights from the fire trucks speeding down the hill toward them.

You're too late, she thought, *they're all gone*.

"Shit!" Bradley yelled, looking backward as he swam.

Elizabeth felt the water around her rising. She felt her cousin trying to pick up the pace as he swam. She looked back and saw a wave coming for them, but it wasn't like a natural wave. The water was rising with *something* swimming toward them, and it was coming fast.

Elizabeth screamed when something popped up beside her as if her heart wasn't beating fast enough. It wasn't what was coming for them, however. It was much smaller, significantly less frightening, and equally afraid of the wave of the unknown as she was. It was a turtle, larger than any she had seen at the local pet stores, almost the same size as Elizabeth, and it was swimming to shore alongside them.

Elizabeth looked back to the wave again, and it was much closer, only feet away now. The wave opened up, and Elizabeth was now staring into a gaping mouth.

Bradley screamed in her ear and let her go, pushing her forward.

With her quickest reflexes, she grabbed onto the turtle's shell and hoped, wished, that it would support her weight while it continued to shore. By the time she felt comfortable upon its back, she had looked back for the wave, and it was gone. There was no sign of her cousin. His screams were now silenced, and she was officially alone. She fell asleep on that turtle's back. The sounds of the waves crashing into shore woke her up. She made it.

Welcome To
CAMP
SAFE
WOODS
PROVIDING A SAFE
ENVIRONMENT FOR
KIDS WHO NEED ONE
LEARN LIFE SKILLS. MAKE FRIENDS. ENJOY NATURE
REGISTRATION ACCEPTED THROUGH JUNE 14TH
More Details Inside